THE PROBABILITY OF EVERYTHING

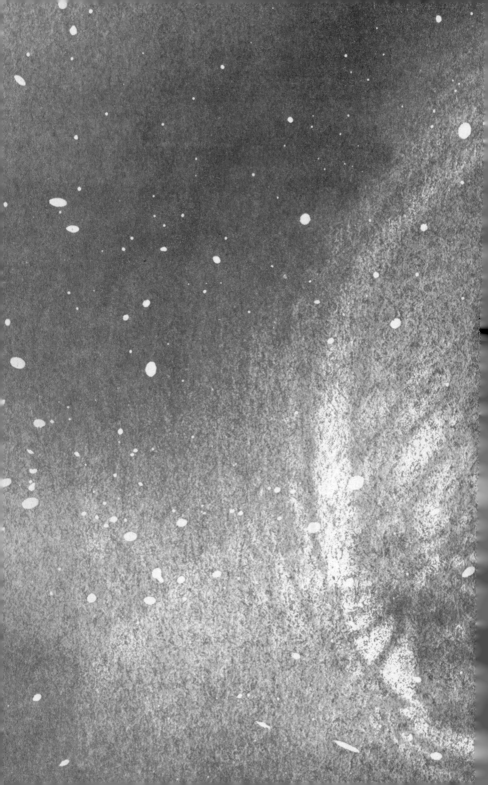

THE
PROBABILITY
OF
EVERYTHING

Sarah Everett

CLARION BOOKS
An Imprint of HarperCollins Publishers

Clarion Books is an imprint of HarperCollins Publishers.

The Probability of Everything
Copyright © 2023 by Sarah Everett
All rights reserved. Printed in the United States of America. No part of this
book may be used or reproduced in any manner whatsoever without written
permission except in the case of brief quotations embodied in critical articles and
reviews. For information address HarperCollins Children's Books, a division
of HarperCollins Publishers, 195 Broadway, New York, NY 10007.
www.harpercollinschildrens.com

Library of Congress Control Number: 2023930370
ISBN 978-0-06-325655-2

Typography by Carla Weise
23 24 25 26 27 LBC 5 4 3 2 1

First Edition

For my birthday twin,
we miss you.

"*W*hen you have eliminated the impossible, whatever remains, however improbable, must be the truth."

—Sir Arthur Conan Doyle

Dear Reader,

If you are reading this, then chances are that our world has ended. I don't know what that makes you. A survivor? Or an alien from another planet, coming to pick through what's left of Earth the way raccoons dig through the trash looking for leftovers? It doesn't really matter who you are. All that matters is that you've found this. All that matters is that you now know we existed.

My name is Kemi Carter, and I'm a scientist. You are probably picturing me now in a white lab coat and goggles, playing with bubbling green solutions in beakers and test tubes, but that's not the kind of scientist I am. For one thing, I'm eleven. The other thing is that there are many different ways to be a scientist. The only requirement is to practice science, and that means gathering information and trying to know more about the world.

My favorite type of science is the science of probability. Probability is pretty great because it tells you how likely something is to happen or not happen. It is a way of predicting the world.

For example, now that you've found this book, the probability that you will read it all the way to the end is 0.5 or 50 percent. That means you have equal chance of reading it or not reading it.

I hope you read all the way to the end because I want you to know everything about how the world ended for us.

I want you to know about our final days. Our last hellos, last I love yous, last goodbyes.

Please don't forget about us.

For your scientific records, I'm going to tell you how it all ends.

Part 1

How the Sun Burned Out

WE FIRST NOTICED THE ASTEROID BECAUSE MY LITTLE sister, Lo, kept trying to eat it.

It was a Sunday morning in April, and the three of us—me, Mom, and Dad—were sitting at the dining table, discussing a news story Dad was reading on his tablet.

". . . the officers spent three hours trying to coax the cat down."

Sundays were the best days because there was no school. I liked school, but I liked being home too. Plus, ever since Dad changed jobs, we all sat down for breakfast together. Dad made pancakes, and Mom and I set the table.

We had the television low in the background as we ate,

and Lo wriggled off Mom's lap, babbling and pointing at the screen. Mom let her hands rest on her round belly, like she sometimes did to include Baby Z in all the stuff we were doing. Dad was talking around a bite of blueberry pancake when Lo started yelling, "Nommy! Nommy!" Which was what she said when she wanted to eat something.

Months ago, when Lo first started saying that, Mom thought she was calling her—Mommy, Mommy—and me and Dad didn't have the heart to tell her the truth, but pretty soon it was obvious that Nommy was just stuff she wanted to put in her mouth. Which was everything.

"NOMMY! NOMMY!" Lo kept shouting.

Mom looked over her shoulder and firmly said, "No, we don't eat the TV, Lo."

We said some variation of that sentence more than twenty times a day.

"No, we don't eat that vase, Lo."

"No, we don't eat the wall, Lo."

"No, we don't eat your sister, Lo."

"No, we don't eat our shoes, Lo."

To be honest, this never worked very well, but this morning, it wasn't working at all.

"Cirque du Soleil is in town next month!" Dad said as he read through the Arts part of the online newspaper.

"NOMMY! NOMMY!"

"I took your mother to that before we got married, Grit," Dad told me, using his nickname for me.

"Lo, I said we don't eat the TV," Mom said.

"NOMMY!"

"You might like that," Dad continued.

"NOMMY! NOMMY!"

"We could all go," I said loudly, so I could be heard over Lo.

"NOMMY!"

"Or the three of us, anyway," I added when the image of Mom shouting *Lo, we don't eat the Cirque du Soleil dancers!* popped into my mind.

It had been a while since we had done anything just the three of us. It felt strange to think that for ten whole years it had been just me, Mom, and Dad, and now it would never be that way again. In just a few months, there would be me and Lo and Baby Z and Mom and Dad. We were like a number pattern where the numbers kept getting bigger and bigger. *1 1 2 3 5 8 . . .*

Lots of things had changed in the seventeen months since Lola had been born. Some of them were tiny, like us having to move the vases Mom made higher up on the shelves so Lo couldn't get to them. Others were bigger, like us moving to Pineview, the "nice" part of Elderton, and our new house never being as quiet as our old one used to be.

"NOOOMMMY!"

Sighing, Dad put his fork down, stood, and walked over to where my little sister was standing. "Want some pancakes, Lo? Yeah, you do."

"No, we don't eat the tele—" As Dad picked her up, his voice stopped abruptly.

"Bim?" He said Mom's name like he was a little bit breathless, like something had knocked the wind right out of him.

Whatever it was in his voice, it made me and Mom both drop our forks and hurry over to where he and Lo were standing in the middle of the living room.

Dad was staring at the television, eyes wide, and as we all faced the screen, it became clear that Lo hadn't been trying to eat the television; she'd been trying to eat the glittering purple circle on our screen.

She'd been trying to eat a planet.

"What's going on?" Mom asked even as a banner of headlines scrolled across the screen.

BREAKING NEWS: MASSIVE ASTEROID ALTERS PATH, NOW ON COURSE TO MEET EARTH!!!

NASA RELEASES STATEMENT: "DO NOT PANIC! PRESS CONFERENCE TO BE HELD IN THIRTY MINUTES!"

It kept rolling out onto the screen, a never-ending treadmill of words that made my heart thump hard in my chest as I stared at them.

"Oh no," Mom said, her voice just as breathless as Dad's.

A sudden chill entered the room. It was a Narnia cold, the kind of cold that makes your bones ache, and I shivered. The front door creaked like it had been left open, and I wondered if that was the reason for the cold.

We had learned about asteroids in Science last year, so I knew that an asteroid was a minor planet, but that was all I could remember about them. I wanted to grab Mom's laptop, curl up on my bed, and find out everything I possibly could about asteroids, but I couldn't look away from the television. My parents couldn't seem to look away either. Dad wrapped his arm around Mom like he wanted to keep her warm, and she put a hand on his chest.

There was now a split-screen on the television, with a journalist interviewing a scientist on the left side and the purple ball—the asteroid—on the other. They were calling it AMPLUS-68.

A short man with twin tufts of white hair sprouting out of his ears pushed a pair of wiry glasses up his nose. His voice was very serious when he spoke.

"Amplus," he said, "has a 84.7 percent chance of hitting us."

"Eighty-four point seven," I repeated under my breath as the ground felt wobbly beneath my feet.

I'm pretty good at math, you see. 84.7 percent meant that the asteroid had much more chance of hitting us than it did of missing us.

When Mrs. Wallace had taught us about asteroids, I hadn't really considered the possibility of one colliding with us. It was kind of the way I hadn't paid too much attention to our lesson on Tasmanian devils because I knew they were only in Australia.

Asteroids were supposed to be in space, far away from us.

Only this one wasn't.

"Thousands of asteroids whiz past us every year and nothing ever happens," said the president of NASA from the left side of the screen. On the right, the planet held steady. "But two hours ago, AMPLUS-68 collided with another asteroid, and then its path changed. We don't have all the facts—where it may hit, how hard it might hit—and until we do, I urge everyone to stay calm."

I did not feel even a little bit calm. I felt dizzy and pukey, like that one time I went on the Big Wheel right after eating two hot dogs at Six Flags. What would it mean for an asteroid to hit us? Would it feel like an earthquake, the whole world quivering underneath us? Or would it be an explosion, one great big BANG before everything went black?

And would it happen today? Tomorrow? In a year?

The thought was too big to wrap my mind around.

"I'm calling Jeremiah," Dad said, reaching for the phone in his pocket.

Jeremiah Woods was Dad's best friend and also the world's leading expert on everything. If there was a new song on the radio, he knew who it was by. If you didn't know how to pronounce a word, he knew both how to say it and where it was from.

I wanted to know what Jeremiah had to say, but I could only hear Dad's side of the conversation.

"Hi, Jere," Dad said into the phone. "How bad is it?"

As Jeremiah talked, my parents exchanged a glance, talking with their eyes like they sometimes did.

I knew then: it was bad news.

The worst news.

The asteroid was going to wipe us out.

Ways the World Could End

I COULDN'T STOP WATCHING DAD'S REACTION TO EVERY-thing Uncle Jere must have been saying. Dad's face was serious and sad, and sometimes he nodded like he'd forgotten Uncle Jere couldn't see him.

"Kemi," Mom said, taking my attention away from Dad's phone call. "You're shaking."

I looked down at my arms and saw that they were covered in goose bumps.

"It's so cold," I said, and my voice was hoarse the way it sometimes got when I'd gone hours without speaking.

"Why don't you put on a sweater?" Mom suggested, a

little distracted because she was also trying to listen to Dad and Uncle Jere's conversation.

Instead of going upstairs, I went to the coat closet and pulled on my puffy winter jacket. Then I shut the front door and went back to the living room. I didn't want to miss anything that happened next.

"Mom," I said when I came back.

Mom tore her gaze from Dad and looked at me. She was biting her lower lip like she did when she was upset about something.

"84.7 percent is a lot," I said, because as freezing as it had suddenly become, it wasn't just the cold that was making me shiver. There was an asteroid hurtling toward our planet, and I was so, so scared.

I wanted my mother to tell me I had it wrong, that actually 84.7 percent did not mean what I thought it did, but she didn't. Her voice was full of so much sadness and all she said was, "I know."

For one second, I wished I were small, that I could be like Lo, who was running around the living room with no worries in the world except what she could eat next. But actually, maybe small wasn't the best thing to be during a collision of planets. Would Baby Z be born before the asteroid hit? Mom was only five months pregnant, which meant the world would have to last another four months at least, if we were ever going to meet the baby. We didn't even know if we had four *hours*.

Mom had to be thinking the same thing, with the way she kept her hand pressed to her tummy.

Dad was still on the phone when the doorbell rang and a voice I recognized called into the house. "Bim?"

It was Mrs. Sorensen from next door, and she was already entering our living room.

"Oh my dears! The asteroid!" she said. "Isn't it terrible? It's just terrible."

Mrs. Sorensen was one of our nice neighbors, not one of the ones who muttered under their breath when they saw us or crossed the street entirely. It wasn't everyone in Elderton who was mean, but our neighborhood—Pineview—was full of people who disliked us on sight. But not Mrs. Sorensen, with her short silver hair, who was always bringing us muffins and brownies chock-full of M&M's. I loved when she visited, but Mom didn't because Mrs. Sorensen liked to ring the doorbell once and walk right in.

One time, Mom was in pajamas, had her hair in rollers, and was getting ready for her job teaching art at the community college when Mrs. Sorensen walked in. Another time, Lo had had a poopsplosion and the entire house was a mess.

But this time Mom seemed happy to see her.

"Mrs. Sorensen," Mom said, her voice choked like she was holding back tears. "Can you watch Lola and Kemi?"

"Where are you going?" I asked. My voice was panicked and small, and I felt silly for it, but I didn't want to be anywhere without my parents. What if the world ended while they were gone?

"Be right back," Mom said. Just before she kissed my forehead, Mom looked me in the eye and said, "I love you more than pastel colors."

Love You More was this game me and Mom and Dad played, and because Mom *really* loved pastels, I knew exactly what she was saying: she loved me a huge amount.

"Equal signs," I said, and there was a giant frog in my throat.

I love you more than equal signs.

"Is it Zoomer?" I asked Mom before she could turn away. Everyone in my family had been trying to guess Baby Z's name since we knew Mom was pregnant with a girl. Mom and Dad had picked out a name that started with Z, but they wouldn't tell us what. I didn't really think my parents would name a baby *Zoomer,* but I wanted to erase the line of worry that had popped up right in the middle of Mom's forehead. That line was the difference between things being OK and not OK. If I could make that line go away, maybe the asteroid could disappear too. Maybe everything could go back to the way it had been just minutes ago.

"Zoomer?" Mom repeated, with a slight smile on her face. But the line stayed put. "Not a chance."

Mom picked Lo up from the ground and handed my sister Blue, a grayish-blue dolphin that was Lo's favorite stuffie.

Dad was still on the phone, but he looked over his shoulder at me and winked.

It was an *everything is going to be okay* wink, a *see you soon, Grit* type of wink, and it made me feel a little bit better. Mom and I had things we shared like a love of books and research, but with Dad, it felt like we shared everything else. The same laugh. The same favorite TV show (a renovation show called *Rush It or Crush It*). The same way of feeling such big emotions that sometimes we drowned in them. I could roll my tongue like Dad could, and just like him, I couldn't hear a song I loved and not dance to it.

Now before I knew it, Lo and I were being shuttled out the door. I only just had time to grab my favorite notebook, the one with the penguin family on the cover, from the dining table before Mrs. Sorensen led us across the grass and up the driveway into her house.

Mrs. Sorensen's house was super warm, and I had to peel off my winter coat as soon as I got into her living room. Her house had thousands of little decorations all around it, the kind you find in gift shops at places like Disney World. Trinkets and mugs and trophies.

Mrs. Sorensen kept the TV on, watching news of the asteroid and holding Lo on her hip, while also dialing a number on her ancient house phone. Soon, she was speaking in an urgent tone to the person on the other side.

"Can you imagine? I can't even imagine," she whispered. Mrs. Sorensen was always answering her own questions, which I guess made sense because how could you know what you thought about stuff if you never asked yourself?

I stayed by the window, looking up and searching behind the clouds for AMPLUS-68, but there was no sign of it. Not even a spot in the sky. Outside, I saw Mom's car start to pull out of the driveway. I raised my hand, but she didn't see me, and the worried, pukey feeling came back.

How long did we have until the end of the world?

I knew I wouldn't feel better until I did some research, until I had some answers. Because sometimes the not-knowing made my skin feel like a Halloween costume that was too small for me. Like I was bursting out of myself, and only finding the right answer made me feel like *me* again.

"Mrs. Sorensen," I said in my most polite voice. "Do you mind if I use your computer?"

Mrs. Sorensen looked over at me, eyes big, like she had forgotten I was even here.

"Sure, honey. Of course I don't mind," she said, pointing me in the direction of the old laptop in the corner of the living room. Mrs. Sorensen was now sitting on the couch, talking to her friend still, and using Blue the dolphin to bop Lo on the nose over and over again. Lo kept giggling and trying to grab her stuffie.

When I sat down and turned on the computer, I opened up my notebook, grabbed a pencil, and started my research. The first thing I looked up was "asteroids," and I wrote down the most important things I could find.

* An asteroid is a minor planet
* Most asteroids are in a belt
* Some asteroids have their own moons
* This asteroid is called AMPLUS-68 because of its massive size
* It has 84.7 percent chance of hitting Earth
* Which means only 15.3 percent chance it won't hit Earth

None of those facts answered the questions that felt so big and stretchy in my mind. Sometimes when you're doing scientific research and aren't specific enough, you don't find the puzzle-piece answer—a fact that answers your question exactly right, like a puzzle piece fitting in place.

I searched "What does the end of the world feel like?"

That was the biggest question mark of all. There didn't seem to be one puzzle-piece answer that fit just right, so I did what any good scientist does.

I gathered even more scientific facts about asteroids and came up with theories about what this meant for the end of the world.

FACT 1: The larger an asteroid and the closer it gets to Earth, the brighter the asteroid will look.
THIS MEANS: When the world ends, you see a blinding white light, possibly brighter than the sun.

FACT 2: Near-Earth objects entering the atmosphere can make a whizzing sound, a stormy sound, or no sound at all.
THIS MEANS: The end of the world might sound like a whoosh, like a thunderclap, or like a peaceful silence.

FACT 3: Past asteroids have made the Earth get hotter.

THIS MEANS: When the world ends, you might get a warm feeling, like being wrapped in a burrito hug.

FACT 4: The law of the conservation of energy says matter can change from one form to another, but it can never be created or destroyed.

THIS MEANS: The end of anything (even the world, even us) is just a change. Kind of like water turning to ice or rearranging furniture. We just become something different.

THIS MEANS: We don't have to be afraid.

We Could
Be Dust

Before I logged off Mrs. Sorensen's computer, I checked my email and saw I had a new message from my best friend, Dia. Dia's actual name was Diana, but even her moms weren't allowed to call her that. *Dia* could be the name of a fashion brand, a logo on the tag of a fancy shirt. "No fashion designer is named boring old Diana," Dia always told me.

We'd been best friends since I started school at Pineview Elementary a year and a half ago, but Dia thought I was stuck in the past because I didn't have a cell phone like most kids in our grade. When I'd asked for one, Mom had said,

"You have forever to own a cell phone, but you only have a few years to be a kid."

From: designedbydia@email.com
To: kemi.carter@email.com
Subject: I CAN'T BELIEVE IT I'M SHAKING
ARE YOU OK

Dia always wrote her entire message in the subject of the email. Mostly because she said email was "super ancient" and she claimed not to know how to use it. Also, because she wrote in all caps, Dia always seemed to be yelling.

From: kemi.carter@email.com
To: designedbydia@email.com
Subject: Re: I CAN'T BELIEVE IT I'M SHAKING
ARE YOU OK

Hey Dia,
I'm OK. I've been doing research and
actually the end of the world isn't so scary.
We should think of it as the start of new
things. For Baby Z, it's going to be new
things on top of *more* new things. I can't stop
wondering what I'll be next, like after the

world explodes. Another human? (Probably
not.) An insect? Since there are ten quintillion
(10,000,000,000,000,000,000) insects in the
world, the probability we'll become some sort of
bug is pretty high, right?
Love,
Kemi

I sent the email to Dia, and only had to wait a few minutes for her response.

From: designedbydia@email.com
To: kemi.carter@email.com
Subject: WHAT DO YOU MEAN BECOME A
BUG I LIKE MY SKIN

I wrote back.

From: kemi.carter@email.com
To: designedbydia@email.com
Subject: Re: WHAT DO YOU MEAN BECOME A
BUG I LIKE MY SKIN

Bugs have skin! Well, they have an exoskeleton.
But if you don't want to be an insect, maybe

we could be stars? I read that real actual
stars in space are made up of the exact same
elements as humans, and since everything is
recycled, we could become anything at all in
the universe. What do you want to be?

While I waited for Dia's response, I looked up how
many stars there were in the universe. It turned out scientists weren't exactly sure, but they estimated about three
hundred billion. I figured the probability of us becoming stars was pretty high (because there were so many
stars), but it was less than the probability of us becoming
insects.

I imagined being a star: twinkling and bright and beautiful, lost in space. Alive in a different type of way.

Since Dia was taking forever, I thought maybe she
didn't like the idea of being stars either, so I thought of
other things there were a lot of in the universe, things we
had a high probability of becoming.

From: kemi.carter@email.com
To: designedbydia@email.com
Subject: Re: WHAT DO YOU MEAN BECOME A
BUG I LIKE MY SKIN

We could be dust. Or rain drops.

We could be anything.

I kept thinking about the different possibilities, and *their* different probabilities, and I made a list ranking both.

For example, because Google said there were three trillion trees in the world, I knew the probability of being a tree was higher than the probability of being a star, but lower than the probability of being an insect.

By the time I finished making my list, Dia had written back.

From: designedbydia@email.com

To: kemi.carter@email.com

Subject: THE ONLY WAY I'M BECOMING AN INSECT IS IF I STILL GET TO WEAR MY SOUND OF MUSIC DRESS

From: designedbydia@email.com

To: kemi.carter@email.com

Subject: OOH MAYBE I CAN MAKE US FASHIONABLE EXOSKELETONS

LIST OF THINGS ME AND DIA COULD BECOME AFTER THE END OF THE WORLD (RANKED FROM MOST LIKELY TO LEAST LIKELY)

Water molecules

Dust

Insects

Trees

Stars

Birds

Shoes

Humans

TVs

Dogs

Zero Is an
Even Number

My PENGUIN NOTEBOOK WAS MY FAVORITE PLACE TO
hide. I knew it was a book and technically not a place, but
whenever the world felt too big, I flipped through its pages
and tucked myself into the words that I'd scribbled in there.
After emailing Dia, I'd spent the last hour imagining the
possibilities of becoming *anything at all in the universe*, and
the world felt impossibly big. I made it smaller by looking
through my notebook.

As Mrs. Sorensen watched Lo in her living room, still
whispering on the phone, I focused on the words I'd written in my book on Friday.

Today in math class, Mr. Gracen said that zero is an even number.

I ran my finger over the words as I thought about them. After Mr. Gracen had explained it, I understood that zero was even because it was before one, which was an odd number. But before Friday, I had always just assumed zero was neither odd nor even because it was a special case. An anomaly.

All the other numbers represented something, but zero was the absence of something.

Did the absence of something still mean *something*?

I was flipping through my notebook when there was a knock at Mrs. Sorensen's front door.

"Could you get that, Kemi?" Mrs. Sorensen asked, and I jumped up and walked over to the door.

Before the door was even fully open, someone was gasping and pulling me to their bosom. Like always, the smell of my aunt's thick perfume overwhelmed me. It was supposed to make her smell like roses, she had once told me, which made me wonder why people can't just smell like people.

Mom's sister, my aunt Miriam, was what everyone in our family called Too Much.

She wept at the drop of a hat, had loud passionate arguments with anyone who would listen, and was regularly overcome by the Holy Ghost at Easter services. Then there was the perfume and the hugging. The squeezing tight, hold-on-till-you-can't-breathe hugs.

That day when she came to Mrs. Sorensen's house, she really wouldn't let go.

"Um, hi, Aunty," I said, carefully untangling myself from the world's longest hug.

Aunt Miriam's eyes were red when she stepped back.

"I can't believe this. It's just not right," she said, and I knew my aunt was talking about the way the asteroid was going to change everything.

Aunt Miriam was a therapist, or as my cousins called her a "feelings doctor." I guess because she had a lot of feelings herself, she liked helping other people with theirs. She had just opened her own clinic a month ago. Her and Mom had gone scouting for the perfect location before deciding on the spot in an office building next to Applebee's downtown. A builder had come in, then she had chosen colors and had it painted. Aunt Miriam was so excited for the adventure of having her own clinic, but the asteroid meant she would have a different adventure than she had planned. We all would.

My chest felt heavy and tight.

I thought of Dad, who quit his job in January to Find His Passion, but now with the world ending, he might not get to do that.

Before this year, Dad used to work all the time. He'd come home late, he was always in dark suits, and he never took me to school or picked me up. Even on the weekends, he'd have to "pop into the office." But one day, he came home with his tie loose and no jacket and said he wanted "more from life."

I thought of myself too and how I was never going to grow up to be a scientist.

I was going to become something entirely different. Dust or a flower or a panda bear.

The thought made me giggle, and then it made me sad.

In just one second, the universe as I knew it had blown up.

Soon, it would *literally* all be blown up.

"Grab your things, Kemi," Aunt Miriam said. "You and Lo are coming to my house for the next few days. I think all of us should be together right now."

I wasn't surprised by this because our family always came together for big events. Like the time when Lo was born or when Uncle Steve's orchestra performed for a sold-out crowd in Ann Arbor. Then there were birthdays and Christmases and Thanksgivings. Now that the end of the world was here, there was 0 percent chance that we wouldn't spend it together.

My aunt thanked Mrs. Sorensen, who had finally hung

up, for taking care of us. And then she drove me and Lo across town to her house. The last year and a half since Lo was born, I'd heard Mom and Aunt Miriam arguing a few times over us living in Pineview.

"Why make waves?" Aunt Miriam always asked. "Stay where you're wanted."

But Mom would shake her head. "I'm not going to live my life afraid," she'd say.

I was pretty sure they were talking about the fact that Pineview was a mostly white neighborhood and we were Black. Aunt Miriam seemed to think where we were wanted was anywhere *but* Pineview, and she was right in a way. We definitely fit in better in the other neighborhoods of Elderton.

Just driving to Aunt Miriam's house, I'd already seen way more Black people than lived in our entire neighborhood.

Now as Aunt Miriam unbuckled Lo from the car seat in her driveway, I hesitated. I was hugging my notebook to my chest and holding my coat even though it was so warm out I no longer understood why I'd even brought it.

"Where are Mom and Dad?" I asked, a sudden jolt of worry rushing over me. What if they didn't make it back for the end of the world?

"Just taking care of some things," my aunt said, leading us into her house.

I knew Aunt Miriam's house pretty well because we visited a lot. We'd also stayed here for a couple of weeks nearly two years ago, while our house in Pineview was being finished. As we went inside, I noticed the house's high ceilings, big open windows, and wide wooden stairs. I always thought of it as the grumpiest house in the world because it moaned and squawked and sighed when you stepped on specific parts of the wood. Me and my cousin Lucas sometimes played this game where we would run from one end of the house to the other end and whoever made the least amount of noise won.

Because Aunt Miriam and Uncle Steve had three kids and a golden retriever, Skip, their house was always noisy, full of laughter and talking. Today, though, when we entered, it was quiet.

It sounded empty and sad, and I wondered if this was what the world would sound like without us.

I forced myself to think about zero again, about the absence of numbers and not the absence of me.

Everyone was gathered around the big TV mounted over the fireplace. They were watching more news about the asteroid. I could see the big purple ball even from the doorway. I was pulling off my shoes when the reporter in the gray suit said something I hadn't heard before or seen anywhere in my research: Amplus was *four* days away.

Four days meant less than a full week of school. It meant we would never meet Baby Z, that I would never get to have two sisters instead of one. It meant the world would end on a Thursday.

Four days was so, so close.

As soon as Aunt Miriam set her down, Lo went running into Jen's arms. Jennifer was the oldest of my cousins. She was sixteen, fashionable, and tall with long, black crochet locs she put in herself. When she finished high school in two years, Jen had a plan to move to Hollywood and open a hair salon for Black actors. "Can you imagine *The* Viola Davis just trying to fake cry for an important scene and someone interrupts her to say they don't know how to style her hair? It's sacrilege!" Jen liked to say, which Mom said meant ridiculous or disrespectful.

Jen thought it was both ridiculous *and* disrespectful that her parents always responded with "We'll see what happens" when she talked about her dream because they thought she should become something important, like a dentist or a teacher.

Today, Jen's hair was pulled back from her face and her eyes looked puffy and small. It seemed like Aunt Miriam's family was less excited about our new adventure and more afraid of everything changing.

"Hey, Lo," Jen said, picking my sister up and forcing a

smile. Lo immediately grabbed one of her locs and tried to chew on the ends of it.

"Kemi, you're going to sleep in Tillie's room, okay?" Aunt Miriam said, and I nodded.

Like magic, Tillie appeared beside me and wrapped her two skinny arms around my waist. If six-year-olds could have a job, Tillie's would be following me around everywhere. Well, first it would be collecting things that had no use, and *then* it would be following me around. This really meant that she was following both me and her older brother Lucas around constantly, since the two of us were usually together. "Hi, Kemi," she said.

I squeezed her back because, even if it sometimes got annoying, it always felt kind of nice to be someone's favorite person. I had a secret hope that Baby Z would be a little bit like Tillie when Z was six. (So far, it wasn't looking likely that Lo would be a Tillie type of six-year-old, but I had hope.)

"Dad gave me his keyboard that doesn't work anymore. It has a bunch of letters missing!" Tillie said now excitedly, like the more that was wrong with something, the more she loved it.

"Wow, that's cool," I said. I definitely did *not* tell her that I (and most other people) liked things that worked better than those that didn't.

I hung up my coat in the closet, said hi to everyone else, and looked around for Lucas, but I couldn't see him.

As Grandma flittered around the living room, picking up crumpled tissues that were on the couch and the ottoman and the ground, she said something to Aunt Miriam who was standing near the front door still.

Most of the time, I couldn't understand my grandmother when she spoke, because she made a point of never speaking in English if she didn't have to. Whatever she said now, though, had a half-bossy, half-kind tone to it. Sort of like how my mom's voice got when she caught me reading way past my bedtime.

After Aunt Miriam answered her in Yoruba, Grandma finally turned to me.

"Kemi, what will you eat?" she asked. "Let me make you something."

Grandma wasn't cuddly or warm, like Dia's *nai nai*. She didn't watch cartoons with us grandkids or tell us stories or call us sweetie, even though I sometimes wished she would. But Grandma put her love into things she made, like knitted sweaters, rag dolls, food. It was almost like she thought love should be useful. It should keep you warm or play with you or make you less hungry. She was kind of the opposite of Tillie in that way.

"Rice? Beans? Garri?" Grandma prodded now.

Then, with a sigh, she added, "Pizza?"

"Um . . ." I said, trying to decide. What *did* I want to eat?

Grandma largely did not approve of the eating habits in our family. She thought we ate too much American food and not enough Nigerian food.

She thought we *were* too much American and not enough Nigerian. My mom was Nigerian and my dad was African American, which made me half of both. Grandma seemed to think half Nigerian was too little.

But right then, she looked willing to compromise.

"Anything," she said.

Now that the world was ending, I guess she figured it was okay to eat whatever.

But somehow the decision felt massive, like I could pick wrong or like it was the very last meal I'd ever have.

"Mom, give her a minute," Aunt Miriam said in a muffled voice. She was crying again and a heavy feeling pressed down on my shoulders like a too-full backpack. My research had made me interested in the huge life change that was coming, but I wondered now if I should be more focused on the not-being-me part. All the grown-ups seemed mostly sad about the end of the world.

"Grilled cheese," I said finally, just to give an answer. *Any* answer.

"Okay." Grandma looked so grateful to have something to do that she was smiling as she went to the kitchen.

Aunt Miriam dabbed at her eyes. The way she was crying on and off, like a leaky faucet, made it seem like the end of the world was all bad. She made it seem like preparing for it might be even worse than the end itself.

I wasn't stupid. I knew that the asteroid meant we would die. Or stop being alive, anyway. We would stop being us. But Aunt Miriam made it seem like we would die even before that happened. From the anticipation, the not-knowing, the sadness. The feeling of thinking about all the things we would miss. The feeling of already missing ourselves.

We would be the first people to die from sadness.

(According to my research, we would NOT be the first to die from asteroids.)

Aunt Miriam's tears gave me a kick in the stomach, a determination.

We were *not* going to be the first ones to die from sadness. We couldn't be.

The asteroid was a shock, something that had come with no one's permission and filled our lives with so much not-knowing. Not knowing what we would be afterward. Not knowing who would come behind us.

But there had to be a way to make everyone feel less afraid of the end of the world.

Should I read them my theories? I wondered, because the only thing that could make not-knowing better was knowing. But then I remembered that science doesn't make everyone feel better. For some people, like Mom, it is art that helps. Other people feel better with music. Or swimming. Or petting their dog.

But what would make *everybody* feel better?

I decided there and then that if there was a way to make my whole family less afraid, I was going to find it.

I gripped my notebook and went up the stairs.

A LIST OF PEOPLE (AND ANIMALS) THAT HAVE ALMOST DEFINITELY DIED BECAUSE OF ASTEROIDS, IN CHRONOLOGICAL ORDER

DINOSAURS

Time Period: 66 million years ago

Many scientists believe a huge asteroid collided with Earth millions of years ago. The immediate impact and the changes to the planet (floods, firestorms, weather changes, etc.) caused the extinction of lots of animals, including non-bird dinosaurs.

MORE THAN 10,000 PEOPLE IN CH'ING-YANG, CHINA

Time Period: March or April 1490

A meteor air burst (an air burst that happens when an asteroid explodes as it enters Earth's atmosphere) in Ch'ing-yang caused rocks of up to three pounds to rain down from the sky, killing tens of thousands of people.

1,000 REINDEER IN SIBERIA

Time Period: Summer 1908

The Tunguska explosion is the largest asteroid

impact ever recorded. It happened over the Podkamennaya Tunguska River in Russia. Witnesses said the asteroid looked like a blue fireball and was nearly as bright as the sun. Researchers believe the asteroid was the size of a twenty-five-story building and that it exploded in the atmosphere before ever touching Earth. The force of the blast damaged forests, killed about a thousand reindeer, and might possibly have killed three people.

ANN HODGES (INJURED BUT DIDN'T DIE)
Time Period: 1954
A woman in Alabama was in her house when she was struck by an eight-pound meteorite (an asteroid that has hit Earth's surface) that had split in two. It has since been named the Sylacauga meteorite. Ann Hodges was injured by the meteorite but didn't die.

1,500 PEOPLE IN CHELYABINSK OBLAST, RUSSIA (INJURED BUT DIDN'T DIE)
Time Period: 2013
A twenty-meter asteroid turned into a fireball and struck Earth. The atmosphere absorbed most of

its energy, but it still resulted in injuries to 1,500 people. It also shattered tons of glass and damaged buildings.

US
Time Period: 2023
TBD

What to Wear to the End of the World

I HEARD LUCAS'S VOICE THROUGH THE OPEN DOOR OF THE bathroom upstairs.

"I'm extremely disappointed in you, Skip," Lucas said. "No, don't give me those sad puppy-dog eyes. You're not even a puppy. You're twelve! That's like a hundred in dog years."

As I followed his voice to the end of the hallway, my foot slid on a puddle of water and I just managed to catch myself before I face-planted.

"Lucas?" I said, sticking my head into the bathroom. I scrunched up my nose as something awful and strong filled the air. "Um, what's that smell?"

Lucas was sitting on the edge of the bathtub while Skip was inside it, half-covered in soap suds. The floor of the bathroom was foamy too, the way I imagined it would look if you opened a washing machine before it was done.

"Hey, Kemistry," Lucas said, scratching his nose on his shoulder because his hands were covered in soap. Lucas thought it was hilarious to take my name and make it something science-y, like Kemical Reaction or Alkemi, which was sometimes funny and clever but usually just plain silly. "I'm giving Skip a bath, but he keeps jumping out and running all over the place. He got skunked this morning on our walk."

"He got skunked?" I asked, finding it hard to wrap my mind around the fact that anything had happened this morning that wasn't about a giant ball crashing into our planet. There was no way to walk into the bathroom without stepping in foam, so I just went in, nasty smell and all. Right as I did, Skip leapt out of the tub and ran to me.

"Dang it, SKIPTOPHER!" Lucas yelled in frustration. (Now that I thought about it, maybe Lucas's entire thing was not calling people by their real names.)

I couldn't help it; I knelt down to pet Skip and let him rub his wet nose all over me in greeting even though he smelled terrible. Then I helped Lucas get him back in the bathtub. I sat on one end of the tub while Lucas scrubbed at Skip's fur and explained about the skunking.

"It's possible that I got a little too close to the skunk. Apparently skunks like their 'personal space,'" he scoffed, making quotation marks around the last two words with his hands. "Skunk personal space isn't even a real thing. It's a myth. Like 'fall' or 'me time.' Or 'twelfth second place.'"

I frowned. "What's twelfth second place?"

"It's thirteen! And where I come from, that's last," Lucas said. "Every team at my soccer tournament got a trophy and even though my team came second, so did everybody else. Even the ones who were dead last!"

"Wow, that's . . ."

"Unfair? Heinous? Despicable?"

"I was going to say weird," I said, "but sure to all the other words."

"Thank you. I thought so too."

Lucas continued on about what he called "the injustices of life."

As he talked, I realized that if Dia was spending the last days with her family and I was spending the last days with mine, then we wouldn't see each other. Maybe at all before the world ended.

"Hey, Luc, can I use your phone?" I asked, interrupting him.

Like Dia, Lucas *loved* his cell phone. Lucas had gotten his phone when he turned twelve and he pretty much had it with him from the moment he woke up till the moment he went to sleep. Not because anyone called him (they didn't), but because it was something he was old enough to have that me and Tillie weren't. It was like a badge of honor or something.

"Only because I trust you," he said, first wiping his wet hands on his jeans and then reaching in his pocket and handing me his phone.

I left the bathroom and walked into Tillie's room, which was basically an explosion of purple. There were purple curtains, two purple bedspreads on her bunk beds, a purple lamp, and a purple rug in the center of the room.

I sat down on the bottom bunk and called Dia.

"Oh, Kemi" was the first thing she said. "I changed my mind about the fashionable exoskeleton. I just want everything to stay the same."

I could tell by her wobbly voice that Dia had been crying. Like Aunt Miriam, my best friend was sort of a crier. Even watching someone cry could set off the waterworks.

At school, Dia and I were last-name buddies. Her last name was Chang-Moore, mine was Carter, and we'd been friends from the minute I sat down next to her and Dia said,

"I *love* your braids." The rest of Pineview Elementary hadn't been so nice. Some people probably thought Dia and I were friends because she was different too at Pineview Elementary. She was Chinese American, and almost all of the other students were white. But we were really friends because we were like magnets; we were different, opposite, but we clicked. I could talk to her about the things I loved, like statistics and science, and she could talk to me about the things she loved, like fashion and candy and vintage clothes.

"It's okay, Dia," I said, and then I told her about all the theories I'd come up with for the end of the world.

"Mostly," I said, "I don't think we should be afraid. And I'm trying to think of a way to make everyone feel less sad about everything changing."

Dia blew her nose trumpet loud on the other side of the phone as I curled up on Tillie's bed.

"You're so brave," Dia said.

"What will you wear?" she asked after a moment.

"What?" I had wandered far away in my head, thinking too many things to put into words.

Things like:

How do you make a giant purple ball less scary?

What will happen to my math homework?

Am I going to school tomorrow?

Is anyone?

I asked Dia if she was going and she said, "I think so. Mom says I should."

"But Kemi," she said, steering us back to what she considered the most important issue, "do you need to borrow something to wear?"

While Dia told me her end-of-the-world fashion ideas, I knelt on the ground and pulled out Tillie's box of Miss Celina's things.

My dad called Tillie "sticky fingers" because she had a habit of collecting useless things from random places—old newspapers, a hairbrush without bristles, expired credit cards. I wondered if Tillie saw something extra in them that I couldn't, if she had special X-ray vision for ordinary things that were secretly extraordinary.

A few months ago, Aunt Miriam got sick of finding Tillie's treasures all over the place, so she got an empty box and wrote MISCELLANEOUS THINGS on it. Miscellaneous things meant a mixture of random objects, but Tillie didn't know what that meant, so she called it her box of "Miss Celina's Things." Now, as Dia told me about all the ways fashion could honor a person, I rifled through old calendars and asthma puffers, Christmas cards and a keyboard with mostly broken keys.

"It's all about memory," Dia said. "Obviously if you want to honor Judy Garland from *The Wizard of Oz*, it's all about the ruby-red slippers because they were what she was known for. They're her *thing*."

"If you were going to channel Snow White, you couldn't do it without a red apple. Different objects remind you of different people, see? And if you're going to honor your —"

My brain jerked to a stop, like a go-kart whose brakes had been slammed hard.

"Wait," I said, interrupting Dia. I heard her words again: *different objects remind you of different people.*

Inside me, my heart was starting to pulse in a different way than usual.

"Is it a heart attack?" Dia asked, alarmed when I told her this.

"The probability that someone my age would have a heart attack is very small," I said to reassure her.

She did not seem all that reassured, but I continued saying what I needed to.

"Maybe that's why Tillie keeps stuff. To remind her of people?" I wondered out loud.

Dia made a clueless sound, but I continued. "Different objects remind us of different people, but what if there are no objects left? If the asteroid destroys everything, there will literally be nothing to remember *anybody* by. And that's awful."

"Huh?" Dia was obviously very confused.

"That's why everyone is sad," I explained, because it felt like I had found the puzzle-piece answer to what was so scary about the world ending. "When the asteroid hits, no one is going to remember us. Years from now when visitors from another planet come, they won't know that we ever existed. They'll never know about cars and about electricity and . . . and . . . Mars bars and fedoras."

"Fedoras?" Dia repeated, distressed. "You take that back right now!"

I smiled.

It was good to know that despite everything else that was changing, my best friend and her fashion obsession never would.

Then I thought about it a little more and realized that it couldn't be true that cars and electricity and Mars bars and even fedoras would be forgotten after the asteroid. There were history books and safes and vaults. The next earthlings would remember the important stuff. They would remember all the people who did cool things like Michael Jordan and Adele and Oprah. They would remember Alexander Graham Bell because he invented the telephone and Rosalind Franklin because she was one of the people who discovered the shape of DNA. They would remember Dia's moms, who were filmmakers and had been nominated for an Oscar.

But what about *my* family?

Mom's Color Me vases. Dad's eyes that crinkled when he smiled. The piano concertos Uncle Steve could play in his sleep. The way Skip and Lucas had kind of the same yawn. The way Grandma's Nigerian music made everyone want to dance. Baby Z who none of us knew yet but who had a whole world of things she could have become (apart from acrobatic, which Mom said she already was).

My family hadn't invented anything; we weren't famous or extraordinary. We were just that: my family. So what did that mean for us?

Maybe, I thought, what was scary about knowing when you were going to die was knowing the exact moment you would stop mattering. It was the worst—a heavy, rocks-in-your-bag type of feeling.

But then suddenly a different feeling came over me, a feeling like there had to be another way. I'd felt it before when I'd decided to raise the most money for the food bank in third grade. And when I'd tried to be the first kid to learn the times-table chart in second grade. I think this feeling was the thing that my father called grit.

"Maybe there's something I can do," I said, blinking, as an idea formed in my mind. I tucked Tillie's treasures back into the Miss Celina's Things box.

"What do you mean?" Dia asked.

"There has to be a way to make sure they don't forget all about us," I continued, and I was sure even as I said it that this was what would make everyone less afraid. "Maybe we don't have to go down without a fight."

Facts About Gritstone (Part 1)

GRITSTONE IS A COARSE SORT OF SANDSTONE. SANDSTONE is sedimentary rock made up of sand or rock grains. These grains are composed of minerals like quartz and feldspar. Feldspar is the most common mineral in the Earth's crust. Scientists think it makes up to 60 percent of the Earth's crust. Quartz is the second most common mineral in the Earth's crust. It is sharp and smooth looking, like diamonds or crystals. Gritstone contains other minerals such as calcium, aluminum, iron, potassium, silicon, and magnesium.

Gritstone can be any color: black, brown, clear, gray, green, beige, pink, yellow, red, or white.

There are two stages of formation. The first is where layers of sand settle and cluster, falling out of water or air. This is called sedimentation. In the second stage, all the clusters of sand group together to form sandstone and are strengthened by minerals, which cause the stone to harden.

Facts About Gritstone (Part II)

SCIENTISTS BELIEVE NIGERIA HAS ONE OF THE HIGHEST rates of twins in the world, particularly fraternal twins. Nigerian mothers have a one in twenty-two chance of having twins. In the Yoruba tribe, the odds are even higher: one in fifteen. But this is only true if your mother still lives in Nigeria, and not in Elderton, Michigan.

When she was pregnant with me, the odds of Mom having fraternal twins was one in sixty, the same as just about any Black woman living in America.

Except at the first ultrasound, there were two of us.

Two heartbeats.

Two sets of feet.

Two slightly too big heads for our slightly small bodies.

My parents both cried when the doctor pointed out our separate hearts.

Apparently, even Grandma cried. In Nigeria, twins are considered a special gift from God.

Mom and Dad bought two sets of everything.

Two cribs.

Two diaper bags.

Two of every set of clothes.

We would have been the kind of twins whose parents dressed them exactly the same way, even though he was a boy and I was a girl.

But when we were twenty-seven weeks, about three months before we were supposed to be born, something went very wrong and they had to take us out early. Usually, it's good to be early to things.

To meetings, to church, to school.

But it's not the same being early for life.

Certain parts of you aren't ready.

Based on the pictures Mom and Dad have of us when we were born, these are some things you need for life but don't have when you are born prematurely: Thick skin. Body fat. Eyelashes.

The pictures didn't show it but our lungs and hearts and brains weren't ready either.

Ty was two pounds and one ounce. I was even smaller at one pound and seven ounces.

The chances Ty would survive were about 80 percent, but I had so many problems at the very start that it seemed less likely I would. The doctors didn't have an exact number for my chances.

Sometimes, things are that bad.

The chances that I would be healthy and strong even if I did survive were even lower.

But in the end, the probability of living or dying or needing a wheelchair didn't matter.

I left the hospital four months after I would have been born.

Ty never did.

The fact that I survived is why Dad always calls me his fighter. Why he says I have grit.

Actually, one time in second grade he called me his fighter after I got in a fight with Cayden Parker when he tried to copy off me in math class. I gave Cayden's chair a little bit of a shove while he was leaning back on its two plastic legs. Mrs. Robbins made me write him an apology.

"He was copying *my* answers," I fumed when Dad was tucking me in that night, because how could everyone not see how unfair it was? And then Dad did something that grown-ups almost never did. He changed his mind.

"You're absolutely right, Grit. Your work *is* worth fighting for," he said. "But hurting someone is never okay. So I'll tell you what, you apologize to Cayden, and I'll talk to Mrs. Robbins."

Before he turned off my light, Dad said, "For the record, I'm always on your team. You're my fighter."

Dad's words didn't mean I could stop the world from ending on Thursday. It didn't mean I could stop everyone I loved from being erased like an Etch-A-Sketch.

But being Grit meant I was going to make sure we were remembered, even if it was the last thing I did.

THREE DAYS
Until the End of the World

Perfect Attendance

I WAS ALREADY DOZING OFF WHEN DAD POKED HIS HEAD into Tillie's room to say he and Mom had gotten to Aunt Miriam's. He came over to the side of my bed and kissed my cheek.

"Sweet dreams, Grit," he whispered.

"Love you, Daddy Long Legs," I gurgled, hugging his neck as he laughed, because sleep always made me babbly and happy.

When I woke up on Monday, a flood of information came rushing into my brain at top speed.

Asteroid. Amplus. End of the world. 84.7 percent. Four days.

Three, now.

I sat up straight in bed, slamming my head on the bunk

bed above.

"Ouch!" My forehead stung.

I carefully climbed out from the bed and walked over to the window.

Somehow, I knew even before I opened the curtains that everything had changed. That yesterday when it all felt like a dream, when it all *could have been a dream*, was over. My heart drum-drum-drummed in my chest as I moved the curtains.

I could see it now. AMPLUS-68.

It sat there in the sky, big and round and bright like the sun. Except it was purple and all the light coming from it was purply blue. It felt like the whole world—the trees, the cars on the road, other houses—was slightly tinged with purple. Tillie's room fit right in with outside, I realized.

Tillie was still asleep on the bunk bed above mine, but when I looked at the clock on the wall, I saw that it was almost seven. Almost too late to leave for school! Maybe most people didn't want to go to school during the apocalypse, but I did.

Usually by this time, Mom or Dad would have woken me, but the creak of Tillie's bedroom door echoed throughout the hall when I opened it. The house was still dark.

I was padding down the hall into the bathroom when Aunt Miriam's voice stopped me.

"Kemi?"

She was in a long flowy nightgown, with a silk head tie covering her hair.

"What are you doing?" she asked, reaching for a light switch so she could see me better. Her own eyes were swollen from all the weeping she had done yesterday.

"Going to take a shower," I said.

"A shower?" she repeated, like if I had just said something crazy. "What for?"

Her voice kept getting more and more high-pitched, and I couldn't help the small giggle that escaped. "So I don't smell," I said, and it sounded like I could have added a "duh" at the end. "School is still on."

"Kemi." Aunt Miriam said my name in a confused sort of way.

Before I could answer, a door swung open and Mom stood in the hallway. She was wearing the oversized T-shirt and baggy jeans she always wore to paint, but there was no familiar smell of acrylics around her, no dried colored splotches on her hands.

Her eyes were small stones in her face, like she hadn't slept a wink. Aunt Miriam had said on the drive to her house that the stress of the asteroid meant that Mom would need all the rest she could get the next few days.

"What's going on?" Mom's voice came out husky, and

she cleared her throat.

"Kemi wants to go to school," Aunt Miriam told Mom, like she'd caught me doing something bad.

Mom rested one palm on the doorframe. She was always more tired anyway because of the baby, but it seemed like the asteroid had made it ten times worse. Amplus also seemed to have put a cloud of sad directly over her.

Mom spoke in a low, quiet voice. "Honey, I don't think that's a good idea. We would like you to stay home."

"Because of the asteroid?" I asked, even though I knew. Everything was because of the asteroid.

I suddenly felt angry, a hot rush of blood under my skin. "I don't care about Amplus. I want to go," I said. "Me and Lindsay P. are the only ones who have perfect attendance for the whole year."

"I know, but . . ." Mom began.

"And I want to go."

My aunt was frowning at me, so I focused all my attention on Mom.

The truth was: perfect attendance was pretty important to me but not as important as the end of the world. I wanted to go to school because I thought I might find something there that I could use for my plan. Like a book from the library, maybe. Plus, then Dia could help me.

Mom shut her eyes for a long second, and when they opened again, they were round and watery.

"I'm sorry, Kemi. The answer is no," Mom said, voice shaky. "We need to all be together."

While we can be was how I expected her to end the sentence but she left it there.

Mom made slow circles on her belly, and I had this strange thought that she was sad for all the things Z would never have. Family movie nights and strong arms holding her, being alive with everyone who loved her.

I decided right then that I would include Baby Z in the plan because she deserved to be remembered too.

"I have an id—" I started to tell Mom about my plan, about how I was going to make sure none of us were forgotten by the next earthlings, but then I stopped. How could I say anything until I knew all my plan's definite details? What if they changed?

"Please can I go to school?" I said, giving it one last attempt. "Dia's going."

"*Dia* is not in this family," Aunt Miriam said, and it made me mad because I just wanted to talk to my mom about this. I was used to my aunt having an opinion on everything, but I didn't want her to have an opinion on this today.

"I think you should stay home," Mom said in a tone that told me this was the final answer.

I felt exasperated, a feeling of too much air in my lungs. They were overreacting.

"This isn't home," I said before flouncing off back into Tillie's room.

What I'd said was true. This was Aunt Miriam's house. I would probably never see my own home again, and it wasn't fair. If we all needed to be together because of the asteroid, why couldn't my cousins have come and stayed at our house? It had only been one night but already I missed our warm carpet, the way our house always smelled a little bit like Mom's paint, the way it sounded full of Lo's babbling voice. I heard my aunt and mom talking quietly as I shut the door, and I was sure Mom and Dad would speak to me later about my "attitude" but all I really cared about was making it to school.

I thought about sneaking out Tillie's window and walking to a bus stop anyway, but that would make my parents even more annoyed.

I sighed.

"ACH-OO!" Tillie's sneeze made me jump so high that if I had been on a basketball court, I might have been able to touch the rim of the hoop.

"You scared me!" I said.

"Allergies," Tillie said. She was almost always sneezing or sniffling because of something my aunt called hay fever, but at least she wasn't crying. I didn't think I could take another day of people crying.

I decided that since I couldn't go to school, I was going to get started on The Plan right here. The Plan was this: I was going to make my own Miss Celina's Things box, except instead of having useless things like Tillie's box did, mine would contain the things we wanted to save, the things we wanted to exist long after us. The only problem was I wasn't exactly sure what types of things I wanted people to remember my family by.

After getting dressed and washing my face, I left Tillie in her room, padded down the hall to the study, and turned on the big computer. I was just about to start my research when I heard Lo's voice.

She had stumbled into the study in her favorite pajamas, a dark blue top and bottom that were soft and thick, like towels fresh out of the laundry. With the tiny robe she had over it, she looked like the queen of some faraway land. Except that she was chewing on the belt.

"Don't eat that, Lo," I told her from the computer chair, but she just continued chewing, her big eyes fixed on me.

"Mommy's down the hall. Go and find Mommy," I said, since I was pretty sure Mom was back in Aunt Miriam's guest room.

I was hoping Lo wouldn't come into the room and start getting into all the stuff on the shelves and the piles of papers on the big desk. My sister could be kind of destructive. In the past, she'd ripped the corner off one of the posters in my room, thrown the clothes out of my laundry hamper and stomped on them, and we'd had a few close calls in terms of her eating my homework. Sometimes, I wondered how we were ever going to survive when it was three kids and only Mom and Dad. Who would make sure Lo wasn't eating stuff she wasn't supposed to be? Who would change Z's diaper when Mom was painting and Dad wasn't home? Some types of changes were impossible to imagine, and adding or taking away people was the biggest one. With one of us added, we wouldn't be the same. With one of us missing, we wouldn't be us.

Now, Lo took a few steps into the room, coming in the exact direction I didn't want her to.

Sighing, I reached out my arms and called her toward me.

She was going to slow my research down but better I had a good hold on her than let her roam free.

Lo used her funny waddling run to close the distance between us and I had to try hard not to laugh. Though

Lo was kind of boring, when I saw her toddling around destroying things, it made me think of those movies where a monster like King Kong or Godzilla invaded the planet and started crushing everything. Picturing that in my brain was always funny.

When she was right in front of me, I heaved my sister up into my lap and wrapped one arm around her waist to keep her in place. She smelled sweet, like milk and apricots. I was pretty sure the scent was coming from the thick mop of curly hair on her head.

"I'm very busy, so you have to be good, okay?" I told her in a stern voice, but for some reason it only seemed to make her giggle. I pulled up a search engine on the computer. I'd done a lot of reading on our solar system and asteroids since Amplus showed up, but that wasn't what I wanted information on now. I typed "Things to save when an asteroid hits" but all it did was take me to different pages about how to survive an apocalypse. That was not what I wanted to know, though; surviving was not an option. We would never be ourselves again, and wasn't that what surviving meant?

I tried "Things to put in a time capsule" instead and waited. A time capsule sounded and felt way more official than a "Miss Celina's Things Box."

I heard voices down the hall, so I glanced over my shoulder to make sure that no one was coming. I wasn't doing anything bad, but I was supposed to ask permission before I used the computer. Especially at my aunt's house.

Lo had gotten the end of one of my braids wrapped around her little hand and a sharp pain hit me when she tugged at it.

"Lola!" I said, in an angry voice. "Stop! I mean it."

"Ah mean eet," she giggled, mimicking me.

What if Z was exactly like Lo? What if there were two of them and one of me?

Since Lo was so much younger than me, we had never really become a pair, two peas in a pod, but I wondered if we would have when she got older. I wondered if there was maybe even room for the three of us—me, Lo, and Z—to be one special group, all the same but different. Like the Three Musketeers.

The end of the world meant we would never know.

I held down Lo's hand with one of my arms, then tried to read.

The most important thing to consider when you are making a time capsule is who you're making it for.

I continued reading as Lo wiggled in my lap.

She was about to start chewing on the end of my braid when I stood up, sat my sister on my hip, and carried her down the stairs to the kitchen. I let Lo down to the ground and she made a beeline for grandma, who was sitting at the dining table reading a book.

"Hiya, Kemi," Uncle Steve said. Uncle Steve was a pianist with the Elderton Orchestra. He traveled a bunch for work so I didn't see him all the time, but when he was around, he always made everyone around him happy. He was funny in kind of a dorky way. His blond hair and sweater vests made it hilarious when he did what he called his "white dad dance" to Grandma's Nigerian music. His white dad dance included a lot of flailing, disco points, and raising-the-roof motions.

Just by looking at him, you'd think Uncle Steve didn't fit in with us any more than my family fit in Pineview, but the truth was that he was right at home here. Him and Aunt Miriam looked different on the outside, but I think when you looked closer—when you heard the piano pieces he wrote for her or saw how they had the same weepy reaction to videos of baby giraffes learning to walk—you could tell they were exactly right for each other.

"What's all this stuff?" I asked now, looking at the counters. Every surface in the kitchen was full of groceries, but not just regular groceries. There was so much food that I wondered where it would fit—bags of peas and canned soups, dog treats and bottles of water—and there were bags and bags of toilet paper. So much toilet paper.

"Well, we need it for the next few days," Uncle Steve

said. "And then after . . . you never know what might happen."

As I stared at all the stuff, I understood that Uncle Steve was saying that maybe these things would help us after the world ended.

The thought shook me.

Didn't he know how asteroids work? How almost definitely Amplus would destroy everyone and everything in its path?

Sure, there was a chance it wouldn't hit, but if it did—*when* it did—we were goners.

I started to tell Uncle Steve that all of the things he'd bought weren't going to save anyone, but I remembered something Mom sometimes asked me: "Is that a helpful comment?"

Was it a helpful comment to tell him that the asteroid was going to shatter the whole world and all the bottled water and canned ravioli in the world wouldn't be able to help us? That he had very little chance of staying himself? That if what he became next was a dandelion or a tree or stardust, there would be absolutely no need for cereal?

I decided it probably wasn't very helpful.

As I helped Uncle Steve pack stuff away, I felt my idea—The Plan—growing bigger and bigger in my mind until it was all I could think of.

And this was what I thought: when the next earthlings found what was left of us, when they stumbled on Aunt Miriam's house and looked through the rubble, they were not going to find toilet paper. Even if we weren't extraordinary or famous, they were going to know about my family, about the things that made us happy and the things that made us sad.

They were going to know who we were.

THINGS YOU CAN PUT IN A ~~MISS CELINA'S THINGS BOX~~ TIME CAPSULE

* Photographs of tiny memories with T-rex–size meanings
  (Example: The holiday card where Lo and I are dressed as Thing 1 & Thing 2; the Halloween me, Mom, and Dad went trick-or-treating as different dinosaurs; me meeting Skip for the first time and him drooling all over my face; all the Christmases and Thanksgivings and birthdays)

* Newspaper clippings to remember the kinds of days that shaped the world
  (Examples: the asteroid that made dinosaurs extinct, the moon landing, the sinking of the Titanic, the birth of Gerolamo Cardano (the father of probability), Alexander Fleming discovering penicillin, the write-up about Uncle Steve's orchestra in the *Elderton Review*)

* Books that make your heart squeeze tight
  (Examples: *The One and Only Ivan*, *Charlotte's Web*, *Where the Wild Things Are*, and *Beloved* for Mom)

* Movies and TV shows where your brand of different is what makes you cool
  (Examples: *Akeelah and the Bee*, *E.T.*, *Matilda*, *The Parent Trap*, *The Fresh Prince of Bel-Air* for Dad)
* Cell phones, if you're not a kid/if you're a kid that isn't me
* Foods that won't spoil but might spoil your teeth
  (Examples: Mars bars for Dia, butter popcorn for Mom, Jell-O for Lo, Twinkies for me and Dad)
* Clothes that make you feel tall and confident and/or like a rock star
* A map of Elderton that shows all the places magic happens
  (Examples: school, church, the playground near our house, the library, the gallery that has some of Mom's paintings, the Y where Dad plays pickup basketball, and Dia's pool)
* Letters that remind you love is specially picked words and inky promises
  (See: letters between me and Dia, letters between me and Dad, notes between Mom and Dad)

Accomplices

On Monday afternoon, the day after we found out about the asteroid, we were all still at Aunt Miriam's house. When Mom and Dad came to join us last night, they'd brought over two backpacks full of clothes and underwear for me and Lo. It was kind of shocking that all the stuff I would need for the rest of my life was in that small bag. I would never outgrow my jeans or need new socks or even get my braids redone again.

These must have been the kinds of sad things Aunt Miriam was thinking about because she was crying *again* when I came down the stairs for lunch. I was the last one down because I'd been busy drawing up plans for my end-of-the-world mission. Lo was in Grandma's lap, holding Blue the dolphin, Dad was next to Uncle Steve, and Mom wasn't at the table at all. When I sat on the other side of him, Dad said Mom was taking a nap. It was kind of early in the day for a nap, but I knew the stress of Amplus was making Mom tired. Last year, Mrs. Wallace had to leave even before she had her baby to go on bed rest. Bed rest meant you literally had to stay in bed most of the day, every day, which, now that I thought about it, was exactly what Mom was doing. Carrying a baby inside you had to be even harder than normal when it was the end of the world.

"We need to talk about plans. All the details leading up to the last day," Aunt Miriam said to all of us, shaking her head like she couldn't quite believe this was happening. "Obviously we'll need food."

Grandma nodded solemnly as she fed Lo some pepper soup. She was always on top of the food.

"Jollof rice," Grandma said, like she didn't even have to think about it.

Jollof rice was my favorite Nigerian food. Something didn't feel right about having the food that made me happiest on the last day of my life. I think it was because the last day would not be happy exactly. Not that the world ending was completely sad either. It reminded me of that word *bittersweet*, which meant a combination of good and bad. If I had to, maybe I'd describe the ending of the world as that: bittersweet. Or maybe it needed a whole new word, like happysad.

Happy because of new adventures, sad because of the end of us.

Forever and ever, jollof rice would be the food we ate when the world exploded, instead of the food we ate on birthdays and Sundays and on other special occasions. The thought was happysad.

Across the table from me, I saw Lucas slip Skip a piece of broccoli. Lucas was the pickiest eater I'd ever met, and Skip would eat anything, so they made a good team.

"Music," Uncle Steve said. "The music is . . . important." He cleared his throat once and it seemed like he was trying not to cry as well. "It has to be just right."

Of course Uncle Steve couldn't imagine the end of the world without music. I couldn't imagine facing the end of the world without numbers, without facts and probability and science.

It occurred to me for the first time that the me-after-the-end-of-the-world, the "new" me, whatever I was, might not love math. I might be a fish in a bowl in somebody's house, never wondering just how big infinity was and never knowing that the odds of a person being born with eleven fingers or toes was one in five hundred.

For the first time, it felt like we might lose more when the world ended than just our plans for the future. We might lose what we loved. We would lose who we were.

My mother might never love colors and art and crafts like she used to. She hadn't painted at all since we'd come to Aunt Miriam's. The world hadn't ended yet but already the not-being-ourselves was beginning.

"Everything's going to be okay," Dad whispered and rubbed my shoulder like he could tell how gloomy I was suddenly feeling. My dad had always been good at knowing me, good at understanding how I felt. Some people were experts on rocks or fossils or cars. Some days it felt like my dad was an expert on me. My mom told this story about how whenever I was crying as a baby, Dad would only have to pick me up and speak to me and I'd stop. How he could know just by looking at me whether I was hungry or sleepy or needed a diaper change. Mom called him the "Kemi Whisperer."

"You're not afraid?" I whispered back.

"Not of this, Grit," he said. That made me feel less sad even as a cold breeze wrapped itself around the entire room like a scarf.

We were just finishing up our lunch when the doorbell rang.

Uncle Steve stood and went to get it. Skip jumped up

from beside Lucas's chair and ran for the front door, wagging his tail in excitement.

"Is this really necessary?" we heard Uncle Steve saying to the person at the door. "This has been really traumatic and I don't think now is a good time."

"Can I go for a bike ride after lunch?" I asked Aunt Miriam over the sound of Uncle Steve arguing with a man.

"If you want," Aunt Miriam said, looking kind of sad. Uncle Steve came back in then, pushing his hand through his thinning hair. He didn't say anything to any of us.

After lunch, we had Operation Lunch Cleanup. Like most other Operations, Operation Lunch Cleanup wasn't a real thing. When Aunt Miriam wanted all of us cousins to do something kind of boring, she made up a name for it and made it seem like some secret mission straight from the government. But giving it a name didn't make loading the dishwasher or cleaning the table any more exciting. The only person who still fell for it was Tillie, who clapped her hands together and asked, "Can I be in charge of it?" when Aunt Miriam announced Operation Lunch Cleanup. Jen just rolled her eyes and kept texting underneath the table, and Lucas pretended he didn't speak English.

"Cleanup? Me no comprehende," he said, which made Dad laugh and Jen roll her eyes a second time.

After the fake mission, I grabbed my backpack from upstairs and went to the garage to borrow a bike and start my real mission. Across the street was an elderly couple everybody called Mama and Papa Johnson; they were staring and pointing at the sky. They were staring at Amplus. I waved at them and they waved back.

I was surprised by how warm it was outside, how the air felt heavy and snug. I'd almost brought my coat out with me, but now I was grateful that I hadn't. I couldn't believe the way Amplus kept changing the weather, making it hot then cold then hot again.

I was trying to roll out one of the bikes when I heard someone clear their throat.

I jumped and whirled around to find Lucas, standing in the space between the wall and Uncle Steve's car, his arms crossed over his chest.

"I sincerely want to believe that you just forgot to ask me to join in the supersecret thing you're doing," Lucas said.

"Who says I'm doing a supersecret thing?"

"You have your Supersecret Thing face on," he said, and then pursed his lips out dramatically. If he hadn't been getting in the way of my plan, I would have laughed. He looked like a blowfish.

But I just sighed.

"Move, Lucas. I have to go somewhere."

"It's about your asteroid, isn't it?" he said. His eyes widened. "Did you figure out a way to stop it?"

"There's no way to stop it!" I snapped.

"There is a 15 percent chance it doesn't hit," he said.

"That's not enough," I said. "There's way more chance it hits us. And do you know what happens after that? We're going to die."

Saying the words out loud for the first time made my stomach spin like a Ferris wheel.

I tried to remember my theories: *you don't have to be afraid.*

The end is the beginning of a new adventure.

"It's just sad that no one will remember us after we're gone," I said in a softer voice. "I think that's why everyone is so afraid."

Lucas was quiet for a moment. "So what are you going to do?" he asked.

"I'm making a time capsule," I admitted. "If I save all the most important stuff, the things we love the most, then nobody has to feel so sad about the end of the world. If I save something for Uncle Steve and something for you and something for Jen and something for me . . ."

I trailed off because I had been thinking out loud.

If I saved one thing that was precious to each member of

my family, then something that was part of them—something that they loved—would always be here. It wouldn't be destroyed by the asteroid, and the next earthlings could find it and know about us.

"Cool," Lucas said. "Where do we start?"

I heaved a giant sigh. "I can do this on my own, Luc. Go practice soccer or play with Skip or something."

Lucas looked hurt. "Is that all you think I do? Play?" he asked.

The answer to that was . . . kind of. When I thought of Lucas, I thought of fun. I thought of funny stories and silly theories and hilarious expressions. I thought of mischief and mayhem and things that turned out wrong no matter how hard you tried to make them right.

"I can't risk this going wrong," I said. And there was more than a 70 percent chance that it would if Lucas was involved.

"I can be serious," Lucas said. "I can be helpful."

"Me too!" a voice suddenly said from behind Lucas, who jumped at the unexpected sound. Tillie popped out of a corner of the garage.

"DANG IT, TILLIPEDE!" Lucas shouted. "How many times have I told you not to follow me?"

"I wasn't following you," Tillie said. "I was following Kemi."

"Go back inside and play with your little dolls," Lucas said.

"You go back inside and play with your ugly soccer ball."

"No, *you* go back inside and—"

"Enough!" I said, raising both arms. "If you're going to help me, you can't fight. And you can't tell anyone else. Also, no joking around, no yelling, and no popping up out of corners without warning."

"Okay," Tillie and Lucas said right away, both of them extremely solemn.

"And *I* make the decisions. You listen to me."

Lucas and I usually made our plans together, but this time I had to make sure we did everything right. I couldn't risk my mission being messed up. We only had three days.

Tillie and Lucas both nodded.

"Grab your bikes," I told them, wheeling the one I was borrowing out of the garage. "Let's go."

The Inside
of the Sun

THE BRIGHT PURPLE BALL IN THE SKY LOOKED EVEN BIG-
ger and brighter than it had this morning. Because it was
closer, I realized.

As me, Lucas, and Tillie rode to Patricia's Diner, I wondered a lot of things, like *Is it bad to look right at Amplus?*
Maybe it was like a solar eclipse, where you needed special
glasses so it didn't burn your retinas. I made a mental note
to do some research, to check what other scientists were
saying.

"I know we just ate," Lucas said as we tied up our bikes
at the front of the diner, "but I could go for a big fat burger
right about now."

Tillie sneezed. She'd seen a yellow wildflower on the side of the road and had gotten off her bike to pick it up and tuck it into her bun. Grandma called Tillie's hairstyle "shuku," which just meant that her hair was plaited so every track went up to the middle of her head, where it formed a bun. Almost immediately after she picked up the flower, Tillie had started sneezing and wheezing, but she refused to take it out of her hair. I guessed it was the next thing going in her miscellaneous things box.

"What do you like about it?" I asked Tillie. "Why is it special?"

"It's special because I like it," she said as we entered the diner, touching the flower to make sure it was in place. "And it makes me look like a princess."

"It makes you look like you need a dose of Be-Be-Benadryl," Lucas said, pretending to sneeze out the word.

"What did I say about not fighting?" I asked, giving Lucas a warning look.

He didn't say anything else.

Patricia's Diner was on the north side, the same side of Elderton as Aunt Miriam's house, and like most other places in town that weren't Pineview, it had a mix of people. Black, white, Asian, Latino. It was busy, full of people around Grandma's age having a late lunch or an early dinner. I would have gone to school if Mom and Aunt Miriam had let me, but it still shocked me that people were living a normal life despite the fact that the apocalypse was three days away. Despite the fact that soon we wouldn't be ourselves anymore. Didn't they know that you stayed home and gathered your family close, that you ate jollof rice and made time capsules when there were only three days left till the world exploded?

I wondered if the sky was even purple for them at all; they definitely weren't acting like it was. Maybe some people's sky was always bright and full of light?

Without even meaning to, I felt my hands ball up into fists at the thought. It wasn't fair.

The sky should be the same for all of us, the same shade of blue or white or purple.

I moved through the doorway and looked around for somewhere to sit.

Patricia's Diner had yellow walls that were so bright and intense, they usually made me feel like I was on the inside of the sun. But the walls seemed a little dimmer today, from the glare of the asteroid through the windows maybe.

Patricia's had a jukebox that played music in the corner and old leather booths. The diner was special, the number-one place on the list for my time capsule, because it had the thing I wanted to save the most, the thing that was precious to me.

In a way, Patricia's was where *I* started. It was the place where my mom and dad had first met. Dad was in college and was working here as a waiter when Mom walked in one day with a group of her friends, wearing a summer dress over her flared jeans, which was the way people dressed back then. (I'd seen all the photos.) Dad said he saw Mom as soon as she came inside and immediately thought she was the most beautiful person he'd ever seen. When Dad came to the table to take their orders, he told them the jukebox was playing requests all day and asked each of them what their favorite song was. After Dad delivered their orders to the kitchen, Mom heard her favorite song start playing on the jukebox. It was "Walking on Sunshine." When it finished, Mom went back to talking to her friends until she heard the same song playing again. It was playing a third time when Dad brought their food out.

"It seems like your jukebox is broken," Mom said, smiling as her friends laughed. Dad asked for her number after that and they fell in love.

"Are you really getting a burger?" I asked Lucas now, sliding into a booth. He sat across from me and Tillie slipped in close behind me.

"I absolutely am," Lucas said, sticking his tongue out

as he typed something on his phone. He might be a picky eater, but he ate a *lot*. "Pats diner dot com."

I couldn't believe it! He'd pulled out his phone to look up the menu online.

"You know there are menus right in front of you," I pointed out, but Lucas shushed me and pretended to concentrate, as if reading a menu off a phone required more Deep Thinking than reading a paper menu.

I sighed.

My family used to come to Patricia's Diner a bunch when we still lived on the north side of Elderton. Not really on special occasions, but whenever one of my parents woke up with a craving for salted pancakes with eggs or a strawberry milkshake.

I picked up one of the menus in the middle of the table and looked through it even though I knew exactly what I wanted. One of my favorite things about Patricia's Diner was that everything was named for someone, even the diner itself. On the menu, there was Pete's sundaes and Janelle's meatloaf and Andre's lasagna. It felt like I could have known any of these people, like I might have seen them on the street or in the grocery store or even sitting at another booth at Patricia's. The real Patricia had retired, too old to run the diner anymore, so her daughters were in charge now. I liked that they kept it named after her even though she was no longer here. I liked the idea of things that lasted longer than the people who made them. Diner names and menu items and time capsules.

At this exact moment, I wished I'd come here with both my parents. I missed our routine, Dad sitting across the table from me and me burrowing into Mom's side. Every time we came to Patricia's, Dad used to lean over and ask me what my food item would be if I could have one item on the menu named after me. I changed up my answer every time: chocolate milkshakes, onion rings, hash browns.

"Hello, party people!" our server, a friendly looking Black woman about Mom's age, said. Her name tag said LOIS! "How is everybody today?"

"Good," we all said.

"What can I start you off with?" she asked me. I didn't know LOIS! which probably meant she was new.

"Can I have the sweet potato fries?" I said, because it *had* to be that. Nothing else was right.

While Lucas and Tillie were ordering, I slid a menu off the table and into my lap. Then I bent down, pretending to look for something and slipped it into my backpack.

I knew stealing was wrong, but I told myself it was for a good cause. For the best cause.

The menu was going to be the first item in my time capsule, and it was important because it would tell the next earthlings about the place where everything started. The place Mom and Dad met, the place where there were dozens of names that would never be forgotten.

When I came back up from under the table, Lucas was looking at me, a glimmer in his eyes.

I saw that, he mouthed to me.

I shook my head at him, hoping he got the message not to say anything.

After we had all ordered and LOIS! had gone to get our food ready, I leaned forward.

"When I come here with my parents, there's something we always do," I said. I wondered if it was making it less special to tell Tillie and Lucas about me and Mom and Dad's ritual, but then I decided it wasn't. Something didn't stop belonging to you just because you shared it with other people.

I dug in my backpack for my bright blue wallet. All the money I'd saved up from my allowance was in there, and I fished out some coins.

I stood up and went to the jukebox in the corner of the room. I put in the coins and chose a song: "Walking on Sunshine." By the time I got back to our booth, Tillie was up and dancing and Lucas stood too and twirled her.

I spun and wriggled my shoulders and laughed even though I knew this was the last time I would hear this song before Amplus hit. Dad called that restless feeling, that urge to dance the Can't Stop! Won't Stop! Itch, and I felt it now in the strongest way. I loved this song that was the start of me, the start of one part of my family, so I threw back my head and shimmied even though a bunch of the customers were starting to point and look at us.

This—dancing in the aisles of the diner while we waited for our food—was soon going to be a memory. Glossy and far away, dusty looking like the Polaroid photos my mom had on the fridge of her college days. Soon that would be all we were: a memory.

It was the saddest thought of all the thoughts that were running through my head, but I closed my eyes and danced like we weren't getting closer and closer to the end of everything we knew.

The Birthday Problem

ONE OF THE BAD THINGS ABOUT DAD'S OLD JOB WAS THAT he used to have to travel all the time. He had to go to New York and New Orleans and Montreal and, one time, even to Tokyo. On my tenth birthday, back when we still lived on the north side of Elderton, Dad was in Cleveland for a business meeting. He'd never ever forgotten my birthday, and he'd promised he would be back to take me out to a special dinner that night.

When I woke up, I had a text on Mom's phone from him.

Happy birthday, Grit! It said.

A probability question for you. What are the chances
of sitting next to someone on a bus who has the same
birthday as you? Tell me tonight at dinner. I love you.

The question stumped me at first.

I wrote down all the facts I had about the problem.

* Two people on a bus
* Same birthday
* There are 365 days in a year

My first instinct was that the answer was 2/365, but
something told me that wasn't right.

I kept thinking about the problem the whole day at
school and then after school, even as me and Mom waited
for Dad to come home from Cleveland.

We waited and waited and waited, but when it was nine
thirty and he still wasn't home, Mom brought out one red
velvet cupcake with a small candle shining on top of it. She
sang "Happy Birthday" and asked me to make a wish. I
wished for Dad to come home and tried to smile. Lately,
it felt like I never saw enough of Dad, and I missed him so
much. He felt hard to hold on to, like something that came
and went the way fog did or the different seasons.

After we ate the cupcake, Mom and I climbed on top of

my bed and she read me one of my favorite books out loud, the way she used to do when I was little. The book was *The One and Only Ivan*, except Mom called it "The One and Only Kemi." Mom did that a lot; she changed the main character's name to mine because she said she wanted me to always see myself in books. "Who says you can't go to Hogwarts or Wonderland or Willy Wonka's factory?" she'd say passionately. "Frankly, I think enough with the Charlies and Harrys. How about some whip-smart, kind, funny Kemis?"

It usually made me smile when she said this, but that night I just sighed.

Mom's smile faded and she squeezed my hand. "Does it matter at all that *I'm* here?" she asked in a quiet way.

I felt bad then. Dad was my favorite person in the world, but I didn't want Mom to feel left out or like I loved her less. I just loved her differently. I started to tell her so, but she stood up and began to tuck me in.

"I know he'll make it up to you," she promised, and I nodded, trying hard not to cry.

I fell asleep within a few minutes, but hours later, I woke up to a soft voice in the dark.

"Kemi?" It was Dad.

"Yeah?" I said, and it felt like my heart jumped out of my bed even before I did.

I flung myself around Dad's waist and he hugged me

tight. "I'm so sorry I'm late. Can we still celebrate? I have a surprise for you."

I saw that it was past eleven already. "Okay," I said.

Dad told me to get dressed and then him and Mom were hustling me into the car.

"We have twelve minutes before it's not your birthday anymore," Dad said as he drove. My fingers felt electric with excitement, like something big was about to happen.

I was kind of surprised when we pulled into Patricia's Diner, but it was so inky dark outside that it felt like even breakfast for dinner would be an adventure. The diner was open 24/7, so it didn't matter that it was nearly midnight; a lot of the other tables were full. We found a table and I slid into a booth next to Dad and across from Mom.

"You know what I think we need?" Dad said, standing up again. "A little music."

He walked over to the jukebox, put in a coin, and then "Walking on Sunshine" started playing. Dad held out one hand for Mom and another for me, and we stood in the space between tables and danced, laughing till we were out of breath.

By the time we collapsed back in our seats, it was past midnight, and it wasn't my birthday anymore. But Dad pushed the menu in front of me and asked if there was anything in particular I liked.

As he said this, he and Mom exchanged a knowing glance and a smile.

I thought about getting a milkshake, so I looked at those first, but then Mom suggested I get something a little warmer and a little lighter, since I already had dinner.

I looked at the appetizers and that was when I saw it.

Kemi's sweet potato fries.

I nearly screamed, I was so excited.

"Oh my gosh!" I said.

Mom and Dad laughed.

"You like it?" Dad asked, grinning from ear to ear. I nodded and hugged him. Mom held out her hand to me and we squeezed fingers across the table.

"How did you do this?" I asked, touching the laminated paper menu.

"Let's just say I have an in with some important people," Dad said, and I knew he meant that he was still friends with Patricia and her daughters.

When the waiter came, I ordered the sweet potato fries.

Mom and Dad shared a piece of cherry pie.

As we ate, Dad said, "So, Kemi, did you figure out the answer to the problem?"

I swallowed and nodded. I'd needed some help, and I

had to look some stuff up on the internet, but I was sure I had it right now.

"It's 0.27 percent," I said.

"First, there's the chance that the first person's birthday falls on one of the 365 days in the year, and that is 365/365 or 1," I explained. "Then you have to times that by the chance that the second person's birthday falls on that same specific day of the year, and that is 1/365. So one times 1/365 is 1/365."

Mom made a face. "Now you see why I like art," she said.

Dad shook his head, and he was beaming at me. "That's right, Grit," he said. Then he smiled at me and said, "Happy birthday, baby girl."

It was a few days later that Mom would tell me she was pregnant with Lo. At first, the idea of a little sister had felt so exciting and new that I'd bragged to everyone I knew about it. It was only after Lo was born that it occurred to me that I wouldn't be Dad's baby girl ever again.

Purple Rain

AS WE LEFT PATRICIA'S DINER, THE SKY FELT HEAVY, BULG-
ing with clouds. It seemed like any second it might start to
rain. I wondered what that would look like. Would there be
purple raindrops, leaving inky puddles all over the streets?

The thing about living in a purple world was that
everything felt possible. Even the craziest things, like flying frogs or cows ice-skating.

Tillie was in a chatty mood as we unlocked our bikes
from the rack in front of the diner. "So can I put my ballet
dress in the t-i-m-e capsule?"

I had specifically forbidden everyone from calling it
a "Miss Celina's Things" box, because that made it sound

childish and lame instead of grown-up and important. It was our time capsule, our Mission.

"Or maybe I could put in my t-u-t-u?" Tillie suggested.

Unfortunately, she seemed to think that the best way to keep our mission secret was to spell out random words in every sentence she spoke.

"Well . . . maybe," I said, thinking, because I was making up the rules as we went along. At the start of The Plan, I had decided to pick everyone's objects for the time capsule, but now that Tillie and Lucas were involved, maybe it was only fair for them to choose the precious thing they wanted saved. In fact, wouldn't it be better if *everyone* got to pick what was precious to them?

"Stop laughing, L-u-c-a-s!" Tillie said.

Lucas just laughed harder and tucked the flower into Tillie's bun, so it stuck out less. "Hey, mastermind? Most people actually do know how to spell."

"Don't call me mastermind," Tillie said. She obviously didn't know what the word meant, but because Lucas had said it, she was immediately suspicious.

"Genius," Lucas teased.

"Stop," me and Tillie said at the same time.

"Smarty-pants," Lucas pretended to cough.

"Lucas!" she squealed.

"Einstein?" he tried.

Before Tillie could get more worked up, I glared at Lucas. "Enough." Even though Lucas was a year older than me, I usually had to be the serious one, the let's-get-it-done-or-else one.

"I'm giving her compliments!" he protested.

"Maybe don't spell out the mission, Till," I said as nicely as I could.

We were walking our bikes across the parking lot when Lucas suddenly stopped.

"Um, why did someone just send me a picture of tennis shoes with the letters *D-i-a* written in glitter? And what's OOTD?"

"Kemi said no spelling!" Tillie complained.

"Dia!" It took me a second to realize the text had to have come from my best friend, and then I leaned over my bike to see Lucas's phone. "OOTD means outfit of the day."

"She just sent another text!" He squinted and turned his phone to the side. "Is that a *cape*?"

Lucas gave me his phone.

"Why do you get more texts on my phone than I do?" he asked glumly.

I scrolled up and saw that Dia had sent several messages. She had probably realized that the best way for us to keep in touch while I was at my aunt's was through Lucas's phone.

KEMMIIIIIIIII, the first text said.

Another: SCHOOL IS THE WORST WITHOUT U!

Then another: HOW ARE WE EVEN SUPPOSED TO LEARN WHEN IT'S THE APOCALYPSE?

OH! THESE ARE THE SHOES I'M WEARING #OOTD

Finally: I WANTED TO WEAR THIS CAPE TOO BUT MOM SAID IT WAS "TOO MUCH." SHE FORGOT THE WORD "AWESOME" AT THE END. IT'S TOO MUCH AWESOME.

I realized now that Dia didn't just email in all caps; she texted like she was shouting AT MAXIMUM VOLUME AT ALL TIMES.

"Can I text her back?" I asked Lucas.

He grumbled something about how much more popular he was in the fifth grade, and I took it as a yes.

I wrote back to Dia: Those shoes are so . . . sparkly!

Dia wrote back immediately: THANK U I KNOW

Me: What are you learning at school?

Dia: BORING STUFF. MR. GRACEN MAKES ME SLEEPY!

For the second time today, I wished I were at school, learning all the "boring stuff" Dia hated, instead of trying to find and bury the things my family loved the most. I wanted to ask if Lindsay P. was there, keeping up her perfect attendance and if they had learned something else as life-changing as zero being an even number.

"Can I keep your phone for a bit?" I asked Lucas.

He sighed and brushed his hand over his face like it was

the hardest decision in the world. "Usually people who want access to my phone have to sign a contract."

"A contract?" I repeated. "I didn't sign anything yesterday."

"I made an exception," Lucas said. "But you're right, we have no pens or paper here."

He heaved a sigh again.

"Fine, but try not to, like, walk and text or anything. And don't make sudden movements! You're more likely to drop it that way. Oh, and if you even think about touching it with greasy hands, you might as well give it back now."

I wanted to laugh because Lucas didn't even carry Lo with this much care, and she was practically a baby.

We got on our bikes, and I only texted Dia when we stopped because Tillie spotted another flower she wanted to smell (and then spend the next ten minutes sneezing from) or because Lucas needed to check that I hadn't dropped his phone.

Dia: I THINK MR. GRACEN SHOULD WEAR A CRAVAT

Me: What's that?

Dia: A KIND OF POOFY NECKTIE

She sent a picture of a white man with sideburns wearing a kind of poofy necktie.

Dia: IT'S EXCELLENT FOR PEOPLE WITH SHORT NECKS

Dia: SHOULD I TELL MR. GRACEN?

Me: No!

Dia: SHOULD I JUST BRING HIM ONE TOMORROW?

Me: Dia! NO.

I wasn't a text yeller, but Dia had me writing in all caps.

Dia: I'M TRYING TO HELP HIM

Me: His neck isn't that short

Dia didn't write back until we were almost on Aunt Miriam's street.

Me: Dia?

Dia: I TOLD HIM

Dia: I HAVE TO STAY IN AT RECESS

Me: Oh no!

Dia: IT'S OK. I CAN USE IT TO CONVINCE HIM TO WEAR A CRAVAT!!!

The Smell of Sadness

WHEN WE GOT BACK TO AUNT MIRIAM'S HOUSE, THERE were a ton of people over. Some of them were people I recognized; others I hadn't seen before. They were all talking in quiet voices, but I heard one man explaining to Aunt Miriam how a past asteroid he'd lived through was so similar to the one currently in our sky. He'd seen the shape before, he said. The purple haze, its blinding light.

"You just gotta keep going," he said in a firm voice, and before I could stop it, my chest squeezed with hope.

Could we . . . live through this asteroid? Could we survive it?

But then I remembered how big Amplus was, how we hadn't had time to prepare or come up with a plan.

I shook my head and whispered under my breath, "We're doomed."

Aunt Miriam's house was big but full of so many bodies that the living room looked small and uncomfortable, like a too-tight sweater. It also had a weird smell today, but I couldn't figure out what it was or why it smelled that way.

Lucas took back his phone, and he and Tillie disappeared into the living room, saying hi to all the guests. I couldn't find either Mom or Dad. I tried to slip upstairs without anyone noticing but it was too late. Susan, Mom's best friend from work, had seen me and then the whole group was descending on me, making a fuss over me. My parents' friends always did this, but they were particularly unbearable today because of the whole end-of-the-world thing.

I hated the way they were all looking at me. It was like this one time a few summers ago when I had too much candy and threw up all over myself right before the wedding I was supposed to be a flower girl in. Just like that day, their eyes were ringed with pity for me.

Remember what it was like to be twelve? She'll never know what it feels like. That's what their looks said. *Twelve should be middle school and pancake Sundays and getting taller than Mom, then almost as tall as Dad. Kemi is never going to be twelve.*

"I'll be right back," I said, slipping away from the group of grown-ups and hurrying up the stairs. When I opened the door of Mom's room, it took a second for my eyes to adjust to the darkness and then I found my mother, a hump in bed sitting against the headboard.

"Mom?" I whispered. There were books and pill bottles on the side table and a tray with half-eaten food on the foot of the bed. Bed rest looked *miserable*. Did Mom have to stay in bed until the asteroid hit? What if she never got to hang out downstairs or eat dinner with the rest of us or say goodbye to everyone?

"Hi, honey," she said, her voice small, just like yesterday.

Then something occurred to me, and fear swelled inside me like a water balloon. *What if something is wrong with her? What if it is the baby?* "Are you okay?" I asked, feeling a blanket of thick air close in around me. Except it wasn't warm or soft or nice; it was just . . . sad. And I realized something then: Aunt Miriam's house smelled gloomy, a big overwhelming, end-of-the-world kind of awful. The smell of sadness was murky and soapy, like the white lilies in the wreaths some of the guests brought with them. It was the sweaty smell of human bodies packed in close together downstairs, plus the smell of palm oil from cooking beans and a bit of obe ata for the jollof rice.

"I'm just beat, honestly," Mom said, forcing a smile.

"There're people downstairs," I told her.

I knew she couldn't go down and see them, but I hoped that hearing this would make her face light up. I hoped that it would remind her of all the people who cared and wanted to say goodbye to us, and that the reminder would make her look less like a glum statue and more like my mom.

"I know," she said, her hands playing with a corner of the comforter that covered her legs. "I do want to see them. I just . . . can't."

I knew the reason why, but I asked in a small voice anyway. "Is it the baby? When do you get off bed rest?"

Mom's eyes were black marbles in the dim light. "I don't know," she said, her voice breaking. "This asteroid. How can it be real?"

She wasn't *truly* asking me, but I wracked my brain, thinking of all the science and math and facts I knew. I wanted to give Mom the puzzle-piece answer, something that would feel solid and sure, something like hope. But suddenly it seemed like there was none.

Mom rested her hand on her belly. "All the plans we had, all our dreams for Z, for Lo, for *you*," she whispered. "None of them are going to happen. It's all gone."

Her words were like bulky combat boots stomping hard on my chest.

And then she was crying.

"We want to give you all so much," Mom said. "Time and love and memories."

I could smell the sadness throughout the house, but Mom's felt close enough to touch. I felt it burrowing into me, getting stuck on my skin. I knew I could let the sad cover me, let all the fear of not-knowing take away the parts of me that were excited for new adventures. I could give up on the time capsule and on becoming stardust and on not being afraid, because the sadness about everything we were going to lose was big enough to cover the whole world.

But then, Mom gestured for me to come to her. "Z's doing gymnastics," she whispered, which was what she always said when the baby was kicking. Mom liked to say that each of us felt different inside her. Ty and I were new and timid and strange. "It felt like I swallowed an alien," Mom said. "Or like there were two little fishes inside me." Lo was forceful, a future soccer player, and Baby Z was graceful with precise movements. If there was a beat or music playing, she moved exactly to it.

When I walked over to Mom, though—deeper into the sticky Play-Doh feeling of sadness—something magical happened. I touched her belly and felt Baby Z fluttering under Mom's skin like the wings of a tiny bird. Inside all the sad was something more.

There was no music, but there was a steady pulse under my hand, a drumbeat of hope that Baby Z was making all on her own. It made me smile despite everything, and I wondered if Z could understand us. (I knew babies could hear; my research months ago told me that.) If Z somehow understood about the asteroid, what if her movement was a promise, a whisper of *don't be scared* to me and Mom?

"Are you and Dad naming her Zeetopia?" I asked as a joke. "Or Zebra?"

Mom's soft hand covered mine and she wrinkled her nose. "That's terrible," she said, then added with a small smile, "and wrong."

It felt a little easier to breathe than it had a few minutes ago, and there was a tiny light in Mom's eyes.

"I love you more than pepperoni pizza," I said.

"I love you," Mom said, "more than I hate pineapple on pizza."

I hugged Mom and left so she could get back to resting. It felt like some of Mom's sadness stayed trapped on my skin, but Baby Z's hope clung to me too.

Hope was light and sadness weighed more, but both things felt like mine.

Change of Plans

I TUCKED THE MENU FROM PATRICIA'S DINER UNDER MY bed, but away from Tillie's Miss Celina's Things box so we didn't get them confused. I wished I could be collecting objects for the time capsule, but there were way too many people downstairs and I was sick of all the end-of-the-world misery. So I read one of Tillie's books on insects until I fell asleep and dreamt I was a stinkbug, which was kind of disappointing. If I was going to be an insect next, couldn't I be a dragonfly or a fire ant or a praying mantis?

When I woke up, it sounded like most of the guests had left. I opened Tillie's door and started down the hallway, ready to continue my mission. But before I reached the stairs, I heard a dry, coughing noise. At first, I thought it was coming from Lucas's room, but the sound was a little farther down the hall. The bathroom.

There was a flush and the sound of a running tap. When he opened the door, Dad didn't see me at first, but I noticed there was a layer of sweat on his forehead and a grayish tint to his skin.

I frowned. "Dad? What's wrong?"

Dad's face lit up like it always did when he saw me, and he waved a hand. "Probably something I ate," he said. He was smiling, though, so he must have been okay.

We went downstairs and then out to the balcony, where Dad's best friend, Jeremiah, was drinking a glass of lemonade and looking at the asteroid in the early evening light.

Outside, the air was so clean it was almost sweet. "Hey, buddy," Dad said, and he and Jeremiah knocked shoulders.

"Hi, Uncle Jere," I said. He smiled big and held out his hand for a fist bump.

"How's my favorite goddaughter?" he asked as I held my knuckles close to his but not quite touching. He had short, twisted dreadlocks and a goatee.

Uncle Jere was a surgeon and I used to think the reason he didn't like to hug or shake hands with people was because his hands were precious, that they had to be protected. I imagined that, if he could, he would peel off his hands at the end of the day and stick them in a safe with his keys and money and expensive watch. But Dad had explained a couple of years ago that Uncle Jere had this condition that made him really afraid of germs. I was kind of confused because don't doctors have to be okay with germs? They deal with sick people all the time and have to be good with blood.

"Actually, it's the one job where I can get away with wearing gloves 24/7," Jeremiah told me once. "I'm not squeamish. Just don't touch me."

He joked about it a lot, but I knew his condition made Uncle Jere feel tired and embarrassed sometimes. Embarrassed to be the only one not shaking hands, the only one eating Grandma's eba with a fork, worrying about dirty door handles. It probably felt like something he couldn't escape or change, like living with his very own asteroid that never went away.

Some other things about Jeremiah were that he had known Dad since second grade, he could speak three different languages and he had once come second on a trivia competition on television.

"I was so close," he'd say sometimes, just out of nowhere.

And Dad would laugh and say in a teasing way, "Tell us again *how* close."

I think the regret of having gotten the final question in that competition wrong was kind of why Jeremiah made sure to know so much about everything now. Music, sports, politics, science, movies.

Out on the balcony with my dad and his friend, there was a new chill. I hugged my arms around myself.

"I'm sorry, kiddo. This has to be really hard," Jeremiah said, looking once at the purple ball taking up half the horizon and back at me. "To go through this at eleven. Man."

"Thanks," I said, but it didn't feel like the same kind of pity the other grown-ups had given me earlier. It didn't feel heavy and too big for me.

"How's your mom?" Uncle Jere asked me.

"She's really sad," I admitted, looking between Dad and Jeremiah. "I don't know if she'll be okay, if she will even paint again."

I was surprised at the choked way my voice sounded. If Mom didn't paint, if she didn't laugh and her eyes didn't sparkle and she didn't make any art, who would she be? What if she spent the rest of the time we had in that dark room? What if she was on bed rest until the world ended?

Dad squeezed my shoulder, looking at me with concern.

"Sure she will," Uncle Jere said. "Just give her time."

"Exactly," Dad said. "Your mother's strength is one of the things I love most about her."

"Okay," I said, even though we all understood that

time was the one thing we didn't have. And then, because I was sure both Dad and Uncle Jere would understand, I told them about The Plan.

"I'm making a time capsule."

"Oh yeah?" Dad said, eyebrows shooting up. "What for?"

"Because we're not going to survive the end of the world. Not as us, anyway," I said. "But if some of the most important things about us do survive, then at least we'll still be here. Kind of."

I turned to Uncle Jere. "You can put something in too," I said. "You're family."

Uncle Jere's eyes got cloudy, and he didn't say anything for a moment.

Finally, he cleared his throat and fished in his pocket for his leather wallet. "In that case," he said, "I know exactly what I want to put in."

He rifled through his wallet and then pulled out a small, folded piece of paper. It was a yellowish color that looked like it might have been white once.

"No way!" Dad cried, clapping Uncle Jere on the back. "You still have that?"

"I'm never letting this thing go," Uncle Jere said, smiling, as he carefully unfolded it.

"What is it?" I asked, straining to see. Uncle Jere's name was printed in the right-hand corner.

"It's a boarding pass," Jeremiah explained.

"You have no idea how much trouble that little piece of paper put us through, Grit," Dad said, laughing. Uncle Jere laughed too, like they had an inside joke.

"Did your father ever tell you that we traveled through Europe after college?" Uncle Jere asked.

"Yes, yes. I told her," Dad said, and I nodded.

"Well, we almost didn't make our very first flight because *someone* lost their boarding pass," Uncle Jere said, eyes twinkling, as he and Dad both seemed to remember something. "And by someone I mean me. I lost my boarding pass."

I smiled. Uncle Jere had this funny, loud way of telling stories that made you wish you could have been there, part of the memory. "There was nowhere we didn't search. Lounges, bathrooms, bathroom garbage cans."

"That was *you*," Dad said, laughing as I made a face.

"It was getting close to boarding time and I swore up and down that if I ever found it, I would never lose it again. I would keep it with me at all times. And I've kept my promise."

"Where was it?" I asked.

"That's the best part." Uncle Jere's smile got even wider.

"Don't listen to him," Dad fake-whispered, but Uncle Jere spoke over him.

"Your *dad* had it." Jeremiah's laugh boomed out of the balcony, and I imagined his joy like the wind, drifting through the air and out into every corner of the world. It was like the opposite of everyone's sadness.

"It's a reminder of the best trip I've ever taken with the best buddy I've ever had. I also keep it to remind your dad how he almost made me miss my flight."

"I should have gone to Europe without you," Dad said, but in a way that me and Uncle Jere knew he was teasing.

Uncle Jere held out the boarding pass to me, but I didn't take it. "Are you sure? If you've kept it all this time . . ."

"Nah, it was made for the time capsule," Jeremiah said. "My most precious item, right?"

"Right." I took it, but it felt unbearably sad that our asteroid was forcing Uncle Jere to let go of something he wanted to hold on to forever. Uncle Jere seemed okay with it, though. When someone called him back inside, he disappeared into the house, leaving me and Dad out on the balcony. "What do you think you'll put in the box?" I asked Dad.

Dad was taking so long to think about it that I made some suggestions.

"Your sunglasses?"

"Old pictures?"

"Cravats?" I giggled a little, thinking of Dia.

"Your tablet?"

"I don't know, Grit," he said in an apologetic tone, looking out at the backyard from the balcony. "Nothing jumps out at me."

I thought about it for a while too, and I realized something: Dad needed my help. Because he didn't just need to find one thing; he needed to find *two*. His passion—the great big love he quit his old job to find—and his most precious belonging for the time capsule.

"Dad," I said, gripping his arm tight as an idea grew big in my head. He turned to look at me. "They're the same thing! The thing you love—*that's* what you should put in the time capsule!"

"I'm not following," Dad said.

"Like maybe if your passion is books, we can put your favorite book in the time capsule."

"I can assure you," Dad said with a laugh, "my passion is not books."

That was more likely to be Mom's time capsule object, not my father's.

"But we can find the perfect thing for you to put in the box!" I said, feeling a wave of excitement. "Before the world ends, we can do it together."

Dad looked unsure. He coughed once and patted his

chest like it was tight. "I don't know, Grit. There's a lot happening, and we don't have much time."

"We don't need a lot of time!" How much time could it take to find the thing you loved most? I mean, if you really, really worked at it? Gathering information or data was one of the most important parts of science. Luckily, I was good at it because the time capsule depended on our very best data collection. Dad *had* to figure out what his heart loved before the world ended so that he could put it in the box and make it last forever.

I had planned to spend the rest of the night gathering objects for the time capsule, but helping Dad find the thing he loved meant a change of plans.

"We need to collect data," I informed Dad. "So we need to design an experiment."

"Okay," Dad said, nodding.

"Which means I need my notebook."

Dad's eyes crinkled as he laughed. "But of course," he said.

I pushed open the sliding door that led into the house, and Dad and I entered, ready to get to work.

EXPERIMENT TO FIND DAD'S
TIME CAPSULE OBJECT

PURPOSE: To figure out what Dad should put in the time capsule

HYPOTHESIS: The thing Dad loves the most is the thing he will want to put in the time capsule and save forever.

MATERIALS: My notebook, a pen, Dad, me

METHOD:

1. Brainstorm some important facts about Dad
2. Remember the things he likes to do
3. Do some of Dad's favorite things to figure out what he loves the most
4. Find an object that represents the thing Dad loves
5. Put this object in the time capsule

RESULTS:

To be observed

CONCLUSION:

To be determined

TWO DAYS
Until the End of the World

Game Time

I WOKE UP SUPER EARLY ON TUESDAY BECAUSE I KNEW time was running out. We had just two days until the apocalypse, and I had two very important things to do. One was to help Dad, and the other was to gather everyone else's time capsule objects.

I yawned as I climbed out of bed, rubbing the sleep from my eyes. Last night had been weird, a purple light slipping in through the cracks in Tillie's curtains. When I'd gotten up to go to the bathroom, I'd looked out the window and seen that, for once, the sky hadn't gone completely dark. It had just gotten purplier. I was starting to get sick of the color purple. Especially because the more purple things got, the closer we were to the end.

After I washed my face and got ready for the day, I ran into Dad in the hallway, which was perfect. He was usually the first person in our house to wake up and I guess he was still the first out of everyone in Aunt Miriam's house.

Dad was holding a warm cup of coffee in one hand and his tablet in the other, and I knew he was on his way downstairs to read the news.

"Morning, sunshine!" Dad said brightly. He was wearing a pair of khakis and a polo shirt, which was exactly the opposite of how he used to dress before—scratchy suits and long-sleeve, collared shirts and shiny dress shoes. They were all supposed to make him look like the best version of himself, but I thought the way he looked now—relaxed and happy—was the best version of him.

"Hi, Dad," I said, clutching my notebook. I couldn't help smiling. "I have a plan to help you find the perfect thing for the time capsule."

Dad looked surprised, like maybe he had already forgotten my promise. "Oh yeah?"

"Yep," I said, starting to lead the way down the stairs. "Do you have running shoes?"

Dad scratched his head. "Um," he said, like he was

afraid to hurt my feelings. "I don't think I want to save shoes forever."

I giggled. "No, Dad! You're going to *wear* the shoes while we do our experiment to find the thing you want to save."

"Oh!" he laughed. "Phew! Well, I could . . . borrow a pair of Uncle Steve's?"

Dad downed his coffee, and we found a pair of Uncle Steve's running shoes for Dad and a pair of Jen's running shoes for me. Uncle Steve's shoes were too tight for Dad and Jen's were too big for me, but we decided they would work.

"So I designed an experiment," I told Dad. "And I brainstormed a bunch of stuff I know about you. And we're going to do some of your favorite things to figure out what you love with all your heart."

Dad's eyes were bright. "That sounds like fun."

"It is," I said, leading the way to the garage. I turned on the light and found Lucas's basketball in front of Aunt Miriam's car. "First up," I said, "we're going to play basketball." I'd decided on basketball because I knew Dad liked watching it and I remembered the bumper sticker on his car that said "LeBron is my homeboy." A basketball might be hard to fit in a box, but if it was what Dad loved the most, then I had to find a way to make it work.

We walked out to the driveway, where a hoop towered over us.

Playing basketball with Dad was always fun but hard. I liked that he didn't believe in letting me win just because I was a kid.

When Dad won the game 16-9, he was happy but didn't brag or rub it in like Lucas might have.

"Good game, Grit," he said, then patted his chest as a loud cough jumped out of him.

"Are you okay?" I asked.

Dad sounded a little short of breath when he said, "Let's sit down."

We must have played longer than I thought.

Dad sat on the concrete, legs stretched out, both of his thumbs pressing the sides of his head.

"Is it that thing you ate?" I asked him, remembering how he'd looked a little off yesterday in the hallway.

"Just a headache," Dad said. As we sat in the driveway, we stared at Amplus. I hadn't thought it could get any bigger in the sky, but it had. Now that we'd stopped moving, the chill was starting again.

I wondered about everything that was going to happen to us in the next couple of days. I wondered what our last moments would be, how they would feel, what we would say. The closer it came, the less I cared about our new adventure and the scarier the end of the world felt.

The thought was making me so sad, but thankfully Dad started talking about something else.

"You know, when I was a kid, I used to walk to the park down the road from my house and shoot hoops by myself," Dad said, as I sat on my hands to warm them. "It's tough being an only child, because you have to do everything alone. That was why we were so excited when we found out you were a twin, because you and Ty would have each other."

"Did you ever get sad that Ty didn't make it, but I did?" I asked in a soft voice. It was something I sometimes wondered, whether Mom and Dad would have been happier if my brother had lived instead of me. Dad called me Grit, but what if it was just a name, one that he would have called Ty instead if he had survived?

"Obviously it broke my heart that Ty didn't make it," Dad said, "but I can't imagine what life would have been like if it hadn't been you. I don't even want to imagine it. Bringing you home was the happiest day of my life, though it was maybe one of the saddest too.

"You can feel two things at once, you know," Dad continued. "You can feel brave but afraid. You can feel happy but sad."

"Like the end of the world," I said, remembering the word I'd thought up for the apocalypse: *happysad*.

"Exactly. Plus," Dad continued, "I think you have a little of Ty in you. Just the way you have a little of me in you and a little of Mom and a little of Lo and a little of Dia and your cousins. I am made up of my parents as well, even though they're no longer here. I think you are made up of all the people and things you love."

I thought about it, specifically the part about having some of Ty in me. I wondered how alike we would have been. Would he have liked science and probability too? Would he have liked the same shows and foods and people? Or would he have been totally different, a one-eighty from me?

It was sad that I would never know, but I also felt happy that I was here. I felt happy to be breathing, to have lived the last eleven years. I was so used to being alive, I couldn't imagine what it felt like *not* to be. Was it painful? Was it sad? Was it like drowning or falling or burning? Or did it feel like nothing at all, like blackness, like the number zero?

I didn't know, but I would soon find out. We all would.

A shiver ran down my spine.

"It's okay to be afraid, Grit," Dad said, and I hugged my knees to my chest.

He continued, "But you have to focus on the other things you also are: Hopeful. Strong. Happy. Lucky. Loved. That's what I think about when I'm afraid."

So I tried to do that, to focus on the other things I felt that weren't afraid.

I closed my eyes and felt the cold breeze. I felt the concrete underneath my body. I felt the thick air. I felt alive.

"Dad," I said, opening my eyes a few minutes later. Dad had stood up and was holding out his hands to me. I noticed his fingers were shaking, and I wondered if he was cold too as he pulled me up. But there was something I wanted to know more. "So is basketball it? Do you want to put a ball in the time capsule?"

Dad thought about it for a second and then he looked kind of sad.

"No," he said with a sigh. "I don't think that's the thing I love the most. I mean, I *like* basketball. But it's not my whole life."

"That's okay," I said as we went back into Aunt Miriam's house. "Remember I wrote a whole list of things about you? We'll try something different."

I recorded the result from the first part of the experiment in my notebook. A basketball was *not* the thing Dad most wanted to save.

I realized as I went and took a shower that this whole experiment might be harder than I originally thought. But I was determined that I was going to finish it before the world ended.

After all, there was no way I could make a time capsule without Dad's favorite thing being inside. It ruined the whole point.

No. My box was going to hold the things we *all* loved the most.

I just couldn't waste a single minute.

STUFF I KNOW ABOUT DAD

1. Dad once spun a basketball on *his* finger for eight minutes twenty-one seconds, which is only three minutes and one second from the world record.

2 Dad's nickname is "Jar" and his best friend's nickname is "Jere," so some people (mostly Uncle Steve) call them Jar Jere Binks, like Jar Jar Binks from *Star Wars*.

3. Dad's first job was holding a giant sign beside Donut Hole that said, "Do NUT miss this →"

4. From all his traveling for work, Dad can say hello, I love you, and goodbye in eleven languages.

5. Dad used to be something called a "financial analyst."

6. He loves Mom and me and Lo like whoa.

7. He officially retired from doing our home renovations when he stapled his thumb with a nail gun.

8. Dad's special talent (apart from catching the Can't Stop! Won't Stop! Itch) is making up words to songs he doesn't know.

9. His all-time favorite singer is Prince.

10. Dad once came third in a waffle-eating contest,

but he ate so many he can no longer stand waffles. His top breakfast food is pancakes now. (He says they are <u>very</u> different from waffles.)

11. Dad says he is deathly allergic to mushrooms, which just means he really hates mushrooms.

12. He always guesses who the bad guy is in movies.

13. He likes writing letters by hand.

14. He knows more about me than anyone on planet Earth.

Memento

WHEN I GOT DOWNSTAIRS AFTER HAVING A SHOWER, Uncle Steve was at the kitchen counter, making breakfast. Everyone else seemed to still be asleep. I wondered if Amplus was making us all sleep later, changing our patterns because of the differences in light, or whether it was just "summer mode."

"Summer mode," Dia once told me grandly, "is not a feeling; it's not an experience; it's a way of being. It is jeans cut short and platform flip-flops and sleeveless turtlenecks." But to me, summer mode was just that lazy feeling you got that made you want to sleep in whenever there was no school. Summer mode had made me late to science camp twice last summer.

I sat down at the island and peeled a banana.

"Ah, Kemi," Uncle Steve said when he turned around and saw me. "Just the superstar I want to see."

I smiled. "Hi, Uncle Steve."

"I heard you're making a time capsule!" he said, half facing the stove and half facing me at the counter. "That is an absolutely brilliant idea, by the way. Inspired."

"Who told you?" I asked as I took a bite of my banana.

"Tillie did. Actually, she spelled it," he said, laughing a little.

I sighed. It didn't need to be a secret anymore, but it still kind of frustrated me that Tillie had told.

At least she hadn't said it was a Miss Celina's Things box.

"Anyway," Uncle Steve said, turning off the stove and walking across the living room to the baby grand piano. He picked something off the top of the piano and came over to where I was sitting. "Your aunt Miriam and I want you to put this in there for us," he said.

"What is it?" I asked, frowning. If my aunt and uncle were going to put anything in the time capsule, I'd have thought they would put in some CDs or sheet music, a journal or a yoga mat. Something musical for Uncle Steve;

something a feelings doctor would like for Aunt Miriam. But Uncle Steve was holding a pair of lime green socks and a plaque with four birds on the same wire. Underneath the birds, it said, *Birds of a feather flock together.*

"Our mementos."

"Your . . . mementos?" I repeated.

"Mementos are keepsakes," Uncle Steve said. "Precious things that belong to us and remind us of a particular time."

As I took the plaque and nearly fluorescent socks from Uncle Steve, I tried very hard not to wrinkle my nose. The plaque was okay, but it was just . . . who put socks in a time capsule?

"They're very bright," I said politely.

Uncle Steve laughed. "That's like pointing out the sun is sunny."

"What do the socks remind you of?" I asked, careful not to add, *Other than stinky feet.*

That was all they reminded *me* of.

"Well," Uncle Steve said, smiling from ear to ear, and I realized something: my plan was working. The time capsule was already making my family happier, and I hadn't even buried it yet. Uncle Jere had seemed glad to give me his boarding pass, like he knew it would last longer in my time capsule than anywhere else. "The socks are from your aunt's and my wedding day. In all the fuss over the big day, getting the suit and the decorations and the cake, I totally forgot about socks! Between you and me, I don't think the world was ready for that much ankle. Your father kindly took the ones off his feet and gave them to me right before I went to stand at the altar. Unfortunately, even back then, Jared had the most spectacularly bad taste in socks."

I smiled because Dad *did* own some terrible socks. I should have put that on the list of facts I knew about him.

"That makes more sense," I said, even though it was still kind of odd to pick socks (ugly or not) as your precious, keep-forever item.

"And the plaque?" I asked.

"A gift from your parents to me and your aunt. It was the first thing we hung up in our first house. Your dad and I were both only children, and when all four of us met, it felt like we had found our wolf pack, to mix metaphors."

I giggled. "You're in a wolf pack?"

"Oh, yeah," Uncle Steve joked. "We're a whole circus troupe. A herd of elephants. A caravan of camels?"

Aunt Miriam came downstairs then and kissed my cheek. "Did you give them to her?" she asked Uncle Steve as her flowery scent trailed after.

"Sure did," he said.

As my aunt and uncle talked about breakfast, I took the socks and plaque and went up the stairs to store them under my bed in Tillie's room. I found a blank sticky note, wrote "KEMI'S TIME CAPSULE," and stuck it on the plaque so Tillie wouldn't mix it up with her stuff. I went back down the hall to Mom's room.

Dad was in the shower in the bathroom next door, and I could hear him singing a very screechy opera song through the closed door. Because Latin was not one of the languages he knew some of, Dad was singing, "A-ve Mariiiiiiia, *something la la la la la LA.*"

I smiled as I opened the door of Mom's room and went inside, climbing into the bed beside her. Lo must have been with Grandma, but I suddenly wanted to hug my mom tight so that all the love I had inside me could fill her up.

"Kemi?" Mom said, blinking awake. She held her arm out and I wrapped my arms around her. Her round belly was between us, but it made me feel like I was hugging Mom *and* Baby Z. We stayed that way for several minutes until the sound of Dad hitting a high note burst through the air.

"Do you think Dad is singing to us?" I asked Mom.

"Man, I hope not," she said, and we both giggled until we cried.

Mom having to be on bed rest for the end of the world was the worst. I missed seeing her around Aunt Miriam's house, missed her kiwi-scented shampoo, her laugh, even the dots of paint that used to cover her body randomly like spots on a dalmatian. Mom being stuck up here till the asteroid hit meant so many special things were over. She would never tuck me in again and read to me at bedtime, like I was a little kid. She would never make me the main character of a book again.

"Please be okay," I whispered into her chest.

She smoothed her soft hand over my face and said, "I love you more than frozen yogurt."

Her voice sounded dry and rough.

"I love you more than hula-hooping," I said, because it was the most fun thing I could think of and I wanted Mom to know I loved her *that* much.

"Sometimes I feel like an extra finger or a toe, like a part of you that you don't need as much," Mom said quietly. I knew she was talking about the times when Dad and I were laughing about something or watching *Rush It or Crush It*, and she'd say, with her hands on her hips, "Anyone care to share the joke?" It didn't happen all the time, but sometimes. Especially before Lo was born.

"But I will be here, whenever you need me, for as long as you do." Mom's promise was a whisper, but there was a strength in it that made me feel a teensy bit better. So I told her about the time capsule, and even in the dark, I could see her eyes sparkling.

"What do you want to put in?" I asked. "What's the precious thing you want to save?"

"So much," Mom said without having to think about it. "Everything."

I waited and she continued, "Pictures, books, clothes, things we made, things we bought."

Mom shut her eyes then, too tired to be more specific, but I could guess what things she really, really wanted. Unlike Dad who found it hard to decide, it was easy to know what Mom loved.

"Okay," I said, and I decided that I was going to get the things she wanted.

So far, I had my *memento* (the menu from Patricia's diner), Uncle Jere's (the boarding pass), and Aunt Miriam's and Uncle Steve's (the socks and the plaque). I still needed Grandma's, Mom's, Lo's and Z's, all my cousins' favorite items, and of course, Dad's.

I had some more plans to help Dad find the object he most wanted to save, but first, I was going to find my mom's mementos. Maybe I couldn't get her *everything* she wanted, but I could get her the important things.

The Forever T-shirt

I HATED CLIMBING OUT OF BED AND LEAVING MOM, BUT IT was all worth it because I discovered something good: Lucas slept with a toy unicorn. His very own stuffie.

I knew this because after I left Mom's room (which was an hour after I played basketball with Dad and showered and had breakfast), Lucas *still* wasn't up. So I went to his room to find him. He was fast asleep, his mouth open, hugging a blue-and-pink unicorn to his chest. And it didn't even look new; it was a little raggedy, like he'd had it a long time. If you had asked me what Lucas slept with, I'd have said his cell phone, so I couldn't help it; I snort-laughed as I looked at him.

He jumped up and threw the unicorn across the room. "How did that get in my hand?"

"Aw, you sleep with a stuffie?" I said.

"No!" Lucas protested. "Unique is Tillie's."

I walked to the corner of his room and picked up the unicorn. Sure enough, there was a name embroidered on it: UNIQUE.

"Unique the Unicorn," I said.

"It's pretty clever, right?" Lucas said, then quickly added, "I mean, I named her, but she's still Tillie's."

"Okay," I said, like I believed him even though I 100 percent didn't. "So you *don't* want it to be your time-capsule memento?"

"It's not even mine," Lucas lied, not answering my question. He wouldn't meet my eyes.

"The time capsule is the safest place for anything precious," I pointed out as I sat at the foot of his bed. "It's the only place where we can save things. And your mom and dad already gave me their mementos."

Lucas looked torn. "Fine," he said with a sigh. "Unique can go in the time capsule."

I wanted to tease him about how much he cared for "Tillie's stuffie," but instead I said, "I need a ride somewhere."

"Somewhere, like, in the country or . . . ?" he asked, one eyebrow going up.

"To my house," I said. "I have to pick up some other stuff for the time capsule."

"Your house is all the way across town," Lucas pointed out.

"I know."

"It's not safe."

"Well . . ." I said, biting my lower lip.

"And we don't drive," he said.

"I know," I said. Lucas was making some very good points. Some very plan-ruining points. I buried my face in my hands.

"However . . ." Lucas said, and even without seeing him, I could hear the grin in his voice.

"Yeah?" I said, dropping my hands.

"You know who just got her license, right?"

Jen was already awake, redoing her crochet locs in front of her mirror. Jen was so good with hair that she sometimes did not just my hair but Mom's, Aunt Miriam's, and Tillie's hair. She would have done Z's too, if Z ever got to be big enough. Thanks to the asteroid, Jen was never going to get to open her salon, but I guess when the world ended, she wanted to go out looking good.

"No" was the first thing she said as soon as Lucas started speaking.

"If you could just—"

"Nope," she said.

"Because I think you—"

"No way."

"What I'm saying is we—"

"Absolutely not."

"WE NEED A RIDE," I shouted when I realized this back-and-forth could continue for the next hour.

Jen looked at me. Even though she was older than me by five years, my oldest cousin and I always got along pretty well. She babysat me a lot growing up and we had this thing where she'd say, "Tell me again who the Greatest Artist of Our Generation is," and I'd say (obviously), "Beyonce."

And then Jen would say, "And who introduced you to her?"

And I'd say, "You" or "My favorite cousin" or something like that. (Personally, I was pretty sure half the reason Jen loved her was that Beyonce always had fabulous hair.)

Jen was particularly obsessed with guessing what day Beyonce was going to drop one of her surprise albums. On random days, Jen would text me (on Mom's phone) to say, "What's the probability that Queen Bey puts out a new song tonight?" Sadly, I usually had to tell her it was pretty low.

(The math goes like this: first, we have to assume that she's even putting out an album this year. Statistically, she puts out an album every three to four years. So let's say the odds that it's *this* year are 1/3.5. Then there's 365 days in a year, and then the probability that it's this or that specific day is 1/365. So 1/3.5 x 1/365 is 0.078 percent which is really, really low.)

"Where are you trying to go?" Jen asked now.

"I need something for the time capsule," I said. "I don't want to ask any of the grown-ups because they're all so busy, planning for the end of the world and everything."

The truth was that I had a feeling my parents would say the time capsule wasn't worth going all the way across town for or Mom would try to pick an object that was already in Aunt Miriam's house to save us the trip. But the thing was: If the objects weren't things my family truly loved, then what was the point of saving them?

"A time capsule?" Jen said slowly. "I can't take you home, Kemi. You do know your house is . . ."

I cut her off, my voice wobbling a little. "I just want to keep our treasures safe."

Jen stared at me, thinking for several seconds, and then she understood. She knew about treasures, things you bundled up in Bubble Wrap to protect. Because dreams and future plans, like styling hair for the movies, were kind of similar to treasures; you had to keep them safe from breaking like glass, keep them safe from people who thought they were silly or not important enough, keep them safe from asteroids.

Jen sighed. "You owe me," she said.

I grinned. "Thanks, Jen."

"How come when Kemi says it you agree, but when I try to, you won't even hear me out?" Lucas grumbled.

About half an hour later, me, Jen, and Lucas were pulling up onto my street and it looked . . . like some place I'd never seen before. For one thing, all the houses looked more similar than ever before. Then there were all the people. There were about ten of them standing at one corner of the street, holding signs about the end of the world.

"REPENT! FOR THE HOUR IS NIGH," one said.

"AMPLUS-68 = THE END," another said.

"THE ASTEROID IS A GOVERNMENT HOAX" and "SEND US TO VENUS" and so many other signs that I didn't have a chance to read them all as Jen slowly drove past. Yellow-and-black tape held back some of the protesters. A couple of people were chanting with their fists raised, but I couldn't hear what they were saying. Lucas whipped out his phone to take a video.

Apart from the trip to the diner, I hadn't been out of Aunt Miriam's house since right after the news of the asteroid. I'd never imagined that people were reacting so strongly to it. I hadn't really *thought* about how other people were reacting, to be honest. I thought for sure they'd be sad, but these people seemed almost . . . angry.

I'd heard a rumor that Elderton's mayor lived close to my house in Pineview, but he must have lived right on our street. Was that why they were here? So they could get the mayor's attention? What did they expect the mayor—or anyone—to do about an asteroid? Dad always said that sometimes when people feel scared, they get angry. Were these people just scared?

"I'm not sure about this. Maybe we shouldn't have come," Jen said, sounding worried and looking over her shoulder at the cluster of people we'd driven by. She hadn't finished crocheting her hair so she had a colorful scarf wrapped around her head. "I'm going to turn around."

"No!" I said, surprised at how urgent my voice sounded.

"I'll be quick," I promised, because how could we have come all this way just to go back empty-handed? I *had* to get the things Mom wanted from inside my house.

"I don't know, Kemi," Lucas said, calling me by my name for once. Also, for once, he seemed to agree with his older sister. "This feels like one of those things that will seem like a very, very bad idea later."

"The people are in the street facing the front of the house. If we pull into the alleyway and go in through the back gate, no one will even know we're here," I pointed out as Jen drove past the front of our house. "If we're really fast, we'll be okay."

Jen sighed, but then she did what I'd suggested, pulling into the alley behind our house and driving till she reached our fence.

"You guys have ten minutes and then I'm leaving," Jen warned as Lucas and I climbed out of the car. We hurried into the yard through the gate and ran up to the back door. I put in our house alarm code, and as the door swung open, I was suddenly afraid. What if some of those people out on the street had broken in? What if there was someone inside our house?

But when I stepped through the back door, all that fear evaporated and I felt a wave of homesickness that was so strong it could have knocked me over. It was weird how knowing that you'd have to say goodbye eventually could make you miss a place or thing or person, even before they were gone.

Our house looked almost exactly the way it had before Lo and I had gone to Mrs. Sorensen's house. All the food on the dining table was gone, but there were still plates with crumbs on them and some forks and even Dad's very cold, days-old mug of coffee. There were traces of us everywhere—Dad especially, because he'd gotten up early like he always did, and his house coat and exercise bike and wallet and other things of his hadn't been moved.

We had left our house forever, but it didn't seem to know that. It looked like it thought we would be back any minute.

"We have eight minutes," Lucas whispered. He was next to me, staring at our dining room too, at our world without us.

I didn't look into our living room, even though it was right *there*, because I knew the memory of when we'd first seen Amplus would send shivers right up my spine. I knew I'd see Dad's outline, his shadow where he'd gone to pick up Lo. It would remind me of the not-knowing, the scariest moment in my life, the worst feeling in the world.

I opened my backpack, pulled out my penguin notebook, and did something I rarely ever did: I tore a page from it.

"Here," I said, handing the piece of paper to Lucas. "Find as many things on this list as you can."

"You could have just texted me a picture of the list," Lucas said, then pretended to remember something. "But wait . . . oh, right! You don't have a cell phone."

I rolled my eyes and started walking away from him.

"House slippers?" Lucas read from the list I'd given him, sounding disappointed. "I thought you'd have crown jewels, diamonds, or . . . or *a golden scepter*."

I was going toward the back door already, but I called over my shoulder to him. "A golden scepter won't fit in a time capsule."

"Wait, but you *have one?*" Lucas asked. Even though I didn't see him, I heard him bustling through the house already, looking for the items on my list, and I felt grateful for his help. Grateful that I didn't have to be in my empty house alone, and that he was taking this mission as seriously as I was.

My plan was to join Lucas in hunting for the items on my list, but first there were two very important things I had to find.

The garden shed was dark and dusty, with the lawnmower in one corner and a bunch of tools, shovels, and rakes next to it. But in the right back corner of the shed, exactly where I knew I'd find them, was a pile of shoeboxes. Some people collected seashells or buttons or mugs, but my mother collected shoeboxes, especially colorful ones. Before Lo was born and back when Dad worked a lot, one of me and Mom's favorite things was to go around town, stopping at all the different shoe stores where they knew Mom by name. (Well, mostly, we went to shoe stores that weren't in Pineview because the shop owners there were less friendly.) We called them our shoebox hauls.

"Bim and Kemi, my favorite two shoppers!" The

manager of Happy Feet said the last time we were there, before disappearing into the back of the store and coming out with all their extra shoeboxes. Mom and I left there with our arms loaded, as other customers stared at us wondering how we could have bought so many shoes. They didn't know that the boxes were completely empty.

Mom made paintings and drew. She sculpted and did pottery, but the projects she loved the most were her Color Me vases. Mom's Color Me Vases were vases she made herself, then decorated with papier-mâché using the cardboard from the shoeboxes. The vases were bright and beautiful, and were all over our house, on windowsills and cabinets, with fake and real plants inside them.

Mom mostly made art for us and for our house, so she definitely wasn't famous—at least, not the kind of famous you needed to be to be remembered.

Now, I reached for the biggest box I could find, feeling a little guilty that I was taking one of Mom's shoeboxes that she could have used for her art. I almost didn't do it, but the thing was that a shoebox was the perfect container for a time capsule. It wasn't too big and not too small. It could be buried in the ground pretty easily, and it didn't cost a lot of money. All I had to do was fill it with the most important things I wanted the next earthlings to know about us. I pulled my backpack off my shoulder and stuffed it inside.

I wasn't sure how much longer we had until Jen got sick of waiting, so I raced across the grass back inside the house. I went up to Mom and Dad's room, opened their closet, and rifled through the hanging clothes until I found it.

The forever T-shirt was Dad's from college. It was a plain white T-shirt with the words "Love, always" on it with a picture of train tracks crossing over each other so they formed an X. When I pulled it off the hanger, I saw that the bottom hem was fraying and there were tiny smudges of paint on the front. I tucked the shirt into my backpack quickly because Lucas didn't know about it. Not even Dia knew about the shirt.

The thing about the forever T-shirt was this: it was magic.

Not the kind of magic that makes you fly or shoot cobwebs or speed-read a book (I tried), but it was magic all the same. Most people thought scientists like me only believed in things we could see, things we could hold in our hands, but actually science was made up of so much you couldn't hold—theories, hypotheses, statistics, equations, formulas. The things you couldn't hold on to sometimes helped to understand the things you could.

The forever T-shirt belonged to Dad's dad before it belonged to Dad.

Dad said he first noticed when he was homesick at college that he always felt better when he wore the forever T-shirt, so he'd kept it for all these years. But the real magic happened a few years ago when Mom started wearing it to paint. First, all her paintings were better. Second, if she was tired or sad or sick, she always felt 80 percent better when she wore the shirt. And then I'd started wearing the shirt, and it always made me feel so warm and loved and calm. Even Lo had gotten the honor of wearing the shirt. It was obviously way too big for her, but some days, when she was in a bad mood, Dad or Mom would slip it over her head and pretty soon she'd either be napping or laughing. I didn't know what made the T-shirt magic. Maybe it was where it was made or what it was made of, but I knew that it worked.

We called it the forever T-shirt because Dad's dad had had it a super long time before he passed it to Dad and Dad said he planned to pass it on to me and Lo and Z someday, so we could share it with the people *we* crazy-loved and it could go on forever and ever. I didn't really know how that would work because all five of us crazy-loved the same people: each other. I loved my aunt and my cousins and Dia, but it didn't seem right to give them the forever T-shirt. Who would I ever crazy-love enough to share this secret, special magic with? I didn't think my heart could fit any more people.

I stopped in my room just to be in it one last time, to touch my pink-and-white comforter, to see the table where I liked to do homework, to see the bed where I'd had the best dreams and the worst.

The glow-in-the-dark stars Dad had stuck on my ceiling years ago were bright because I had my blinds closed and the room was dark. I had exactly five stars up because Dad said they were supposed to represent us. Me and Mom and Dad and Ty and Lo. Now, I stood on top of my table and used a marker to draw a sixth star on the ceiling, the grainy plaster making it a little wonky-looking. But it was for Baby Z.

When Mom and Dad first told us about her, I'd thought there would be so much time for Dad to put another of the plastic stars up, but time had run out. It was too late.

I knew some stars could come in pairs, like me and Ty did, or they could come in other multiples. They were linked together by gravity, and they orbited around each other.

I thought of us like that, a family of stars, and I wondered what hope we had against the massive asteroid hurtling toward us. Were asteroids bigger than stars? Or were stars bigger than asteroids? I wasn't sure, but I made a mental note to look that up later.

I thought about taking a star down, for the time capsule, but I couldn't bring myself to do it. The six of us belonged together, and here, we could be together forever. Or at least until the end of the world.

I went into Mom and Dad's room. On their dresser mirror was the newest ultrasound photo of Baby Z. In it, her right leg was extended a little bit, her toes pointed.

"Show-off!" Dad had joked about the fact that the ultrasound showed how graceful she was going to be. Mom had written **"Meet Baby Z!"** on the bottom of the picture my parents used to tell everyone that Lo and I were getting a baby sister. I could have let Z's memento be one of the bibs or socks or tiny onesies that Mom had gotten from the guests at her baby shower. But the next earthlings would never know my littlest sister. They would never know if she was loud or quiet, if she was funny and a big eater like Lo, if she liked math and science like I did. There was so little we knew about Z, but I liked this shadowy image because it was a picture of all of her. It was every itty-bitty cell and organ in her itty-bitty body, and that one pointed baby foot gave the future earthlings so many stories they could tell about her.

Ballerina, tap dancer, gymnast, poised, fancy, elegant.

If people could tell stories about you, then you would

never really be gone. You could never be forgotten.

I looked around at the rest of my parents' room and imagined that I was cocooned between Mom and Dad the way I used to be on stormy nights when I was little and snuck into their bed. I used to feel so safe that way, like nothing could hurt me. Mom and Dad seemed so big, like they could cover me with their bodies and their kisses and their words. I thought they were the kind of extraordinary that would never stop or end or die.

Now, I knew there were things that were bigger than Mom and Dad. I knew that there were asteroids and natural disasters and sicknesses and all sorts of things that meant we had never been safe, that we never would be safe. At any moment, anything could knock us out of the sky and change us forever. And my parents weren't extraordinary in the big ways other people were. If we were going to be remembered, I had to make it happen.

I hurried downstairs to find Lucas and help him look for the last few items on the list. When it was time to go, I was feeling pretty good about how the time capsule would turn out.

We locked the back door and were almost at the fence when a man with a bushy beard stepped out in front of us. He'd followed us into the yard! Someone must have seen us pull into the alleyway.

The man's eyes were wide and scary in a way I couldn't explain.

We tried to pass him, but he blocked us with his body.

"Not so fast, children," he said with a deep voice, towering over us. He smiled from ear to ear like we were friends, like he knew us, but I'd never seen him before in my life.

"Um, BioKemistry?" Lucas whispered. From the corner of my eye, I saw him digging in his pocket for his phone, like he wanted to call someone for help but he couldn't seem to find it.

And that's when I knew we were in trouble.

Ambush

THE CAMERA CAME OUT OF NOWHERE AND WAS SO CLOSE to me that the glass lens was almost touching my forehead. Another man appeared and pushed a microphone in front of our faces. A third man was shouting questions, and all of them were crowding us.

"Do you kids live on this street? In this house? What are your names?"

I opened and shut my mouth. These didn't look like the angry people at the corner of the street—these people were different. And somehow, scarier.

Lucas found my hand and clutched my wrist.

"What do you know about the end of the world?" one man asked.

"How do you *feel* about the end of the world?" the other said.

"I . . ." I started, but my mouth was dry and no words came. Lucas wasn't speaking either.

"Have your parents explained what's happening to you?"

"Are you afraid of AMPLUS-68?"

They were asking so many questions so quickly that I felt dizzy.

I gripped the strap of my backpack with the hand that Lucas wasn't holding.

"What do you have to say about—"

"Hey! Shoo!" Hearing Mrs. Sorensen's familiar voice out of nowhere was so comforting, I could have cried. She was hurrying from her yard into ours, waving a broom like a threat. "Back off, you vultures! Leave those poor kids alone. I'll call the police!"

"We want a child's perspective. Asteroids affect kids too," one of the men said.

"I'll give you a perspective," Mrs. Sorensen said, actually hitting the bearded man in the stomach with her broom.

"Hey!" he cried, surprised and stumbling back.

Mrs. Sorensen swore and swung her broom at one of the other guys, just barely missing.

"Luc! Kemi!" someone hissed under the commotion. Behind the men, Jen waved her arms, signaling for us to come to her.

"But Mrs. Sorensen—" I started to say. We couldn't just leave her, could we?

Before I could argue, Lucas tugged at my hand and quickly led us around the men to where Jen was waiting for us at the gate.

"Omigosh omigosh omigosh," she chanted, panicked, as we ran back to her car. "Are you guys okay? I knew we shouldn't have come here!"

I slid into the passenger seat and Lucas slammed the back door.

"Oh, *here's* my phone!" Lucas said, picking it up from the back seat. He seemed disappointed that he kept his phone so close at all times, but it hadn't been there for him when he'd needed it the most.

Jen backed out of the alleyway quickly and drove us past the protesters again and out of our neighborhood. She heaved a sigh of relief when we'd passed them.

"I told you ten minutes!" Jen said, and she sounded like she was about to cry. I felt like crying too and I couldn't say why. "What did they want with you?"

"They wanted a child's perspective," Lucas said, parroting what we'd heard the man say. "On Amplus."

"Are you okay, Kemi?" Jen asked, looking in her rearview mirror at me. She must have noticed that I hadn't said anything. I nodded.

We were all silent for the rest of the drive and I wondered whether Lucas and Jen were replaying what had just happened like I was, wondering who those people were and why they spoke to us and why they were asking so many questions.

As we drove back, I noticed something I hadn't on our way here: more protesters, police cars in alleys, people with cameras and microphones. There weren't as many as on our street, but they were spread out through the city. The hairs on my arms stood up as straight as a tree.

When we reached Aunt Miriam's house, there was absolutely nobody on her street and relief flooded my body.

I'd spent every day we'd been here missing my house, missing my bed and missing having my own space, but at this moment I was so grateful that we were staying here. Something weird was happening in our town—something to do with the end of the world—and I wasn't sure I liked it.

Instead of thinking too hard about it, instead of trying to find the puzzle-piece answer the way I normally would, I decided that I had to spend the next two days focused on the time capsule and on helping Dad find the perfect object for the box. I didn't have time to worry about what was happening in Elderton or on my street. I did hope Mrs. Sorensen was okay, though, especially since she'd helped us get away from those men with the cameras.

Someone must have called Mom about what happened (maybe Mrs. Sorensen?) because she met us at the front door. I was surprised to see her out of bed, and she looked so small in one of Dad's robes, her hair a tangled mess.

"Shouldn't you be in bed?" I asked, feeling like I needed to reach out and hold her steady, like maybe lying down so much had made her legs forget how to be legs.

"What were you thinking?" she asked, ignoring my question, and I hated the anger in her voice. "I told you we all need to be together. Here."

"I got some stuff for the time capsule," I said, hoping that would make her less mad. "The forever shirt," I whispered so only she could hear.

"That's not important," Mom said, hugging Dad's robe around herself and I couldn't believe she'd said that. "The most important thing is us, and being safe and . . ."

Mom inspected me from top to bottom. "Are you hurt? Was there—"

"She's fine, Aunt Bim," Jen said softly. She still looked shaken by what had happened and also a little bit guilty.

Did Jen think it was her fault for taking us to my house? She would never do me another favor again.

Mom looked at my oldest cousin, then back at me. Finally, she seemed satisfied because she hugged me. "Nobody leaves the house without asking permission."

I tried really hard not to show how disappointed I was or how much this would wreck my plans. What if other people's mementos for the time capsule were outside the house? What if *Dad's* memento was somewhere else, and we couldn't reach the one true thing he loved?

A feeling of panic rose from my chest to my throat. Suddenly, it seemed like I could feel every single second that was slipping away. Every single second that was bringing us closer to the end of the world. I wasn't the smallest bit excited about new adventures anymore or what we all might be after the apocalypse. I was thinking about the ending of all the things I loved and knew and wanted.

Dad came down the stairs then. He walked slowly, holding on to the railing. He was frowning. "Why on earth did you go home?"

"To get some things," I said. Since I didn't want to explain about the forever shirt in front of everyone, I tried to tell him with my eyes that it was something for the time capsule, and actually, I think he got it because he gave me a small smile.

Mom was still standing near the staircase and Dad wound both arms around her from behind. Seeing them standing next to each other, I noticed something I hadn't before: Mom looked tiny and like the bed rest wasn't helping her tiredness. Plus, she looked so, so sad. But Dad's skin was gray compared to Mom's. His lips were dry, and his eyes somehow didn't look like his. They were older and darker. My stomach squeezed tight, and I knew. Something was wrong with Dad.

Was it whatever bad thing he'd eaten a few days ago? Or was it something else?

Aunt Miriam said I could use the computer, so I went upstairs and did some emergency research.

When I searched Dad's symptoms, my heart felt like it was falling, sinking deep into a pit. I wrote down the most important facts I could find.

Fact 1: Nausea, vomiting, and headaches are the first signs of radiation illness.

It all made sense now—the coughing, the slow way he'd been moving, the way he'd been out of breath when we played basketball. Dad was sick because of Amplus.

Fact 2: There is no cure for radiation sickness.

My research said radiation illness could kill people in just a couple of days. It meant Dad might not even make it to the end of the world.

I wanted to cry, because this wasn't fair. This wasn't the plan.

We were all supposed to go together.

I didn't want *any* of us to die.

If we absolutely had to, though—if there was no way we would survive this (and there wasn't)—I hoped it would take us all at once. I didn't want it to be slow and long and hard. I didn't want it to take us one by one, like plucking apples from a tree. That was what I hoped for from this asteroid, what I expected from it: it would hit hard, one time, and take all of us with it. Nobody would be left behind. Then, our new adventures could begin and we could become anything at all in the universe.

"What's up, Grit?" Dad said, appearing in the doorway of the study like he'd known that I was thinking about him.

I jumped up and threw my arms around him, hugging him so tight it was like all the cells in my body were hugging all the cells in his body.

Dad laughed a little, patting my back. "Is everything okay?" He smelled like pine and soap, like Dad.

Did he know he was sick? And if he did, did he know *how* sick?

I couldn't imagine a world without my father. I didn't want to.

So I decided that I wouldn't think about radiation sickness or asteroids or death until I absolutely had to. I wouldn't even bring them up.

"Our experiment," I said, finally letting go of Dad.

Dad smiled at me. "Ah, yes. Do you have something else in store for your old man?"

Hope. Crazy-love and mementos, bright socks and stolen menus. Happy memories and favorite stuffies. These were the things I wanted to think about.

"I have *so* much more," I said.

What's Possible

FINDING THE ONE THING YOU LOVED WITH ALL YOUR heart was much harder than it seemed. Or it was for Dad, anyway. I'd never thought before about how lucky I was that I'd discovered the thing I loved—science and math and probability—without really even having to think about it. I loved probability because of the story of how I was born. But I also loved probability because of Dad.

All my life, I'd always been afraid of things I hadn't tried before. Like roller coasters or new foods or backflipping into a pool. But this one time when I was seven and too scared to go on the Zipper at the Elderton fall carnival, Dad said, "What are the different possibilities, Grit?"

The line for the ride was extremely long and I was taking forever to get onto the ride, but Dad didn't get mad or rush me, even though some of the people behind us were grumbling.

"I could fall out? Or it could crash? Or it could get stuck in the air?"

"Or?" Dad said. "You're missing a big one."

"Or it could be okay, I guess," I said. It was always easier to think of the worst things that could happen.

"Perfect," Dad said. "And how likely is it that you fall out? Or that it crashes? Or that it gets stuck in the air?" Dad held up his phone. "Should we look?"

We looked online and it said in over a million rides, the Zipper had only gotten stuck seven times. No one had ever died on it.

I immediately understood what Dad was trying to say. Based on the past, based on the math, the chances that everything would be okay were way more than the chances that things could go wrong. This didn't mean that things could 100 percent not go wrong (the only time something is 100 percent sure is when it has already happened), but that they most likely wouldn't. The thought made me feel safer, and so much braver.

Since then, I started to think about the probability of everything, the different possibilities and then how likely they were to happen, and it always helped me feel less afraid.

The day before the world ended, Mom was back on bed rest and Aunt Miriam and Uncle Steve were out making some "arrangements" for the end of the world.

I was eating lunch in the dining room, and Dad was playing with Lo while he waited for me. We were about to start today's data collection.

Strangely, Jen was kind of hovering around me while I ate. I wondered if she still felt bad or mad about the trip to my house.

"Sorry for getting you in trouble," I said over the sound of Lo babbling in the next room.

Jen shrugged. "You know the time capsule?" she said, her hands behind her back. "I wanted to put something in."

"Okay," I said, feeling a burst of pride that my idea was good enough that even Jen, even my *parents*, thought it was smart.

She held up a weird big oval thing. When I got closer, I saw that it was one of those signs that lit up in the front of stores. It had the word *OPEN* written in cursive.

"What's this?" I asked.

"The first sign for my hair salon," she said gloomily. "Or what *was* going to be the first sign for my salon. It was a gift. Want to see what it looks like lit up?"

She plugged it into the wall near the table, and the

OPEN glowed with a golden neon light in her hands. It was beautiful and sad all at once.

"Wow," I said.

Jen unplugged the sign and handed it to me. It was slightly warm and heavier than it looked. I felt like I was holding much more than the sign. It felt like I was holding something else I couldn't see, like a dream. My throat was tight, the way it got before I cried, because Jen would never get to open her salon now. She would never get to move to Hollywood, and her new adventure almost definitely would not include being a hairdresser.

"Let me guess, Luc wants to put in Unique?" Jen smirked, changing the subject. She seemed to know that the end-of-the-world sadness was wrapping around me again.

I sniffed back my tears.

"Does everyone know about the unicorn except me?" I asked, surprised because she was right. Lucas *had* given me Unique.

"Pretty much," she said.

The neon sign would be a tight fit in the box, but I went upstairs and put it under my bed with the rest of the growing pile of mementos, the growing pile of things we had to say goodbye to.

When I went back downstairs, Grandma had taken Lo for a nap, so I had Dad all to myself. We decided we would spend the rest of the day going through some of the things on my list for him.

We started with cooking. Since Dad loved to make pancakes on Sunday mornings, I thought there was a very good chance cooking was what his heart loved best, and his memento could be his favorite recipe. Dad and I followed instructions from the internet and made some peanut butter drizzle pancakes, which were pretty much just pancakes with melted peanut butter poured over the top.

Dad had to sit at the counter for most of the cooking because he kept losing his breath, but the pancakes were so delicious. We gave some to Tillie, who had been kind of cranky since she'd woken up to find me, Lucas, and Jen gone this morning. The pancakes seemed to make her forget how upset she was at being left out.

Tillie had stuck the yellow flower from yesterday's bike ride back in her hair. It looked a little limp and tired today. I wondered if being plucked from the ground meant it was dead already or if it was just in the process of dying, the way the rest of the world was.

Every now and then, Lucas would lean over the railing of the landing and yell something that Dia had texted me. It was like he was a messenger between us, a carrier pigeon.

First, Lucas said: "Dia wants to know what you think

about scrunchies and high ponytails? Is it an end-of-the-world lewk?"

I imagined my best friend's yelling, all-caps texts and smiled as Tillie and I cleaned up the kitchen. Dad was too tired to help much, but he kept us company while we worked. My chest hurt thinking of him dying, thinking of him being gone before the world ended. I squeezed my eyes shut to hold back tears and thought of high ponytails.

I said, "Tell Dia anything can be an end of the world look."

Later, Lucas said: "Dia said how about top hats?"

I'd stolen half a pancake while I was drying dishes, and I choked on it. "She wants to wear a top hat on the last day?"

Even later, Lucas said: "Dia says she's thinking a fascinator should be the must-have item for apocalypse season."

Dad scrunched up his nose and coughed. It was loud and dry-sounding. "What's a fascinator?"

Lucas asked, and Dia answered: THOSE TINY FANCY HATS BRITISH PEOPLE WEAR. DUCHESS KATE IS SOOO CHIC.

Finally, Tillie and I were done cleaning up and we sat down with Dad to polish off the rest of the pancakes.

As we sat at the counter, Dad slipped Skip a couple of bites because he had these big pleading dog eyes and peanut butter was his favorite. I also thought Dad might have been feeling too sick for the pancakes.

"So, Dad," I said, desperately wanting to focus on something that wasn't Dad dying. "This has to be the thing you love, right? We can put this recipe in the box!"

Dad thought about it for a second. "I do like to cook, but I feel like are you really a cook if you make exclusively breakfast foods?"

"Yes," I said. Tillie seemed to agree.

Dad grinned, then sighed. "You know as great as this is, it's maybe not the thing I want to be remembered by forever," he said.

It was my turn to sigh. Dad's memento was starting to feel slippery and hard to catch, like a slug or Jell-O.

"I'm sorry, Grit," Dad said, placing a hand on my shoulder. "I understand if you're ready to give up on me."

"Give up?" I repeated, shocked. "Absolutely not. We're just getting started!"

Next up, we watched *Rush It or Crush It*.

While Dad found the right channel, I turned to Tillie. "What do you want to put in the box?"

Apart from Dad's memento, which we were working on, only Lo, Tillie, and Grandma hadn't given me anything for the time capsule. I had an idea what I'd put in it for Lo, but when I'd asked Grandma this morning, she'd said she'd think about it, then kind of waved me off so she could keep reading some recipe books to pick out our last meal.

"You mean in the t-i-m-e capsule?" Tillie asked now. I wanted to tell her there was no point in spelling it, that everyone knew. And even if they didn't, everyone but Lo could spell. Instead, I just nodded.

She wriggled her nose. "I'm still deciding."

"Not your tutu?" I asked. "Or ballet shoes?"

She shook her head.

"How about that flower in your hair?" Dad asked, coming back to sit down beside me on the long couch.

"Yeah," I said. "What about the flower?"

Tillie touched it with her hand. "No," she said quietly, and I knew she was saving it for her miscellaneous things box.

Rush It or Crush It was one of me and Dad's things, and even though I didn't mind Tillie watching with us, I also didn't mind when she got bored and wandered upstairs to play video games with Lucas. *Rush It or Crush It* was this show where the host, Piper Peters, was given only a week to fix a condemned house, to knock down walls and repaint and repair windows, and if she didn't make it in that time, they had to crush it. A condemned house is a house that is in such bad shape that no one can live there until it is fixed. We had started watching the show back in January when Dad left his job.

"I think Piper's got this," Dad said a few minutes into the first episode. Both our feet were stretched out on the ottoman and I could tell Dad was trying very hard to pay attention even though he wasn't feeling the best.

Just make it one more day, I thought in my head.

One more day was the same as making it to the end of the world, and that felt like it would be enough. Just as long as we never had to say goodbye. "It looks pretty bad," I said, trying to focus on the show. "What if they can't get the basement done in two days?"

For the most part, we both believed in Piper, but the best part about watching *Rush It or Crush It* with Dad was that we both tried to guess at the start of each episode whether she would finish on time or not. I liked that there were only two possible endings: the house being rushed or the house being crushed. That every single time there was equal chance—50 percent—of either happening. I loved things you could predict.

"So what are we doing here, Grit?" Dad asked. "You want to know if professional TV watching is my passion? Because I think it could be."

I laughed. I couldn't imagine Dad doing nothing but watching TV all day.

"That's not a passion," I said. "That's a vacation."

Dad laughed too.

I explained the real plan behind us watching *Rush It or Crush It*.

"I thought since you liked this show, you might want to put something in the box that is about building things. Fixing pipes and knocking down walls and tearing out carpet."

Dad made a face. "I can tell you right away that is *not* my passion. The extent of my ability to fix things is changing the battery in the fire alarm, and even that . . ."

I giggled but then remembered the full story and stopped laughing.

One night last December, the fire alarm in our house had started ringing, making Lo cry and waking us all up from sleep. Dad went down and "fixed" it. He'd just crawled back into bed when it started again. Dad went down a second time and stopped it. As soon as he got back upstairs, it started again. I came out of my room and watched as Dad climbed the ladder to turn it off again. "Is it possible this thing gets even louder every time I stop it?" Dad grumbled. Dad was always the first to wake up, but he was usually the first to go to bed too. He said there wasn't an ailment sleep couldn't cure. So seeing him looking all rumpled and cranky made me giggle even though the alarm was majorly disrupting my sleep also.

It would have been a funny story if it ended there.

But Dad had just managed to make it quiet for a third time when there was a loud rapping sound on the front door. Dad sighed and went to get it.

I heard a familiar voice: Mr. Vance, our neighbor on our right side. He was cursing and yelling, saying horrible things to Dad because of the alarm. I pictured his dark brown hair, ice-blue eyes, and the chain with three silver coins that he always wore around his neck.

I listened, feeling a tightness in my chest as Dad apologized and told him to calm down.

"DON'T TELL ME TO CALM DOWN," Mr. Vance bellowed, getting even more worked up and I felt afraid.

"Kemi." Mom came down the stairs, holding Lo. "Go upstairs. Take your sister."

I hesitated because Mr. Vance sounded really angry. What if he said even more awful things to Dad? What if he actually *did* the things he was threatening to do to Dad? I stood at the top of the stairs holding Lo while Mom and Dad talked to Mr. Vance. But he only seemed to get angrier and angrier. He kept saying "people like you" and "you folks" and things that made it sound like he was a separate

176

species from us. Like we were maybe sea creatures and he was a land animal. Beluga whales versus mountain lions.

He seemed especially upset that we'd moved here in the first place, as if we'd come last week and not over a year ago.

The alarm started again and Mom rushed back in, climbed the ladder herself, and did something to make it quiet. This time, it stayed quiet.

By now Mr. Vance had gone, but I didn't know how he and Dad had ended their fight. I wasn't sure I wanted to.

"So we know I won't be contributing a recipe, a basketball, or a tool kit to your time capsule," Dad said now, bringing me back to reality. "What else is on your list?"

"Was there something you *used* to love?" I asked, thinking maybe the key was finding something Dad hadn't thought of in a long time.

"Oh man," Dad said, thinking about it and scratching his head. "I've loved a lot of things in my life. There's an unlimited number of things you can fit in your heart."

"I'm 150 percent sure that my passion will always be probability," I said, even though usually my pet peeve was when people talked like the probability of anything could be greater than 100 percent. One hundred percent is THE MAXIMUM, 0 percent is THE MINIMUM. Still, I made an exception this time since I was so completely sure I would always love the science of predicting the world.

"I don't doubt you will," Dad said, smiling, "but you should keep your mind open—you might surprise yourself."

"Hmm," I said, because I was *positive* my love of probability would never change, but I didn't want to argue with Dad.

"But maybe you're onto something there," Dad continued. "Maybe finding the thing I love enough to save forever will mean looking backward, not forward. Why don't I sleep on it and see what I come up with?"

I was pretty disappointed that we hadn't gotten anywhere tonight, but I agreed. I could tell Dad was asking to stop because he didn't feel good. His skin had gotten even grayer, and his eyes looked so small and tired.

"We'll figure it out tomorrow," I said, instead of what I really wanted to say.

What I wanted to say was *please, please, please don't die before the world ends for all of us.*

What I wanted to say was that if we didn't find the object Dad crazy-loved tomorrow, then we wouldn't be able to save it. The thing he loved most in the world would be forgotten.

Because time was running out.

ONE DAY
Until the End of the World

The End of Things

ON WEDNESDAY, I WOKE UP TO THE SOUND OF SOMEONE calling my name.

I sat up too fast and slammed my head on Tillie's bed again. I would *never* get used to this bunk bed.

Well, I guess I don't really have to, I thought.

"Kemi!" Aunt Miriam called, and I jumped out of bed and hurried out into the hallway.

My aunt was at the foot of the steps, wearing a pink robe with a bouncy Skip by her side. "You have a guest," she said, beaming at me.

A guest?

Aunt Miriam hadn't smiled once since Amplus got here, so whoever this was had to be really special.

I started down the stairs, but before I even got to the bottom, a girl with long straight black hair rushed at me.

"Dia!" I exclaimed. Dia and I hugged, squeezing each other tight. I'd last seen her on Friday at school. Today was Wednesday, but it felt like years—centuries even—since we had seen each other.

"I missed you so much!" I told Dia, finally letting her go because Skip was bopping around behind us. He hated the idea of any hugs that didn't involve him.

"I'm not even joking when I tell you I was literally dying to see you," Dia said, sitting down on the stairs and petting Lucas's dog. "That's why I asked my mom to let me stop by before school."

I paused a little at my best friend's words, and not because she'd used the word "literally" wrong for the millionth time. "You're *still* going to school?"

We were so close to the end of the world. How was school even open?

Dia looked apologetic. "Yeah. My parents made me," she said.

"What's the point of school when everything ends tomorrow?" I asked, a little bit annoyed. I knew it wasn't

Dia's fault that she was going to school. I would have been going too if my parents had let me.

Dia shrugged, her hands still lost in Skip's fur. "It sucks without you. Lindsay P. has been bragging about how she's the only one who has perfect attendance now," she said, rolling her eyes. "As if that even matters."

"It doesn't," I said over the lump in my throat. And I knew it didn't—that when the apocalypse happened, it was not going to matter who won what. Nothing was going to matter. Except.

I'd worked really hard all year to get the perfect attendance award. And now, because of something I couldn't have imagined, I had lost it.

"I'm sorry," Dia said gently. "But, hey! I brought you something."

I noticed as Dia walked down the remaining steps and over to the couch that she was wearing a pair of tie-dye pants that flared out wide at the bottom, a white T-shirt that said FLOWER POWER, and a brown fringe jacket. She hadn't let the end of the world stop her from doing the thing she loved most in the world: dressing up.

Lying flat on the couch Dad and I had sat on to watch TV last night was a long black garment bag. Dia picked it up and held it out to me.

"Don't open it until tomorrow," she said. "Promise?"

I promised her I wouldn't, even though I was bursting with curiosity.

Lucas and Tillie came downstairs then, Lucas yawning in his checkered blue pajamas, holding his trusty phone, and Tillie's dying flower already in her bun again. She sniffled as she came down the stairs.

"Whoa," Lucas said, eyes widening when he saw Dia. Dia was the kind of person who *looked* special. She was beautiful, had these supercool super-round glasses, and wore clothes that everyone had an opinion on. Some of the girls at school, like Lindsay P., thought she was a "show-off," but Dia never let their whispers and stares bother her. She was just expressing herself, just loving the things she loved out loud. Today, her tie-dye pants were especially loud, so it was no wonder Lucas was staring.

Dia had never met my cousins because her and I mostly hung out at school during the week and I usually saw my cousins during the weekends. That is, when the world wasn't ending.

"You're Dia? I'm Lucas." Lucas had finally stopped staring enough to shove his hand in front of her.

Dia stared at his hand before shaking it. "Dia."

Lucas nodded thoughtfully. "But your actual name is Diana, right? So why don't you pronounce it *da-ya?*"

"Because it's *my* name," she said. Dia hated when people gave their opinions on her name. "Plus Dee-yuh just sounds more high fashion."

"Oh, that makes sense," Lucas said, then went quiet, even though "high fashion" was one of those things only my best friend understood.

"I'm Tillie," Tillie said, wiggling her nose like it was itchy and Dia smiled at her.

"Hi, Tillie," she said. "That is such a pretty name."

"It's short for Matilda," Tillie told her, then sneezed.

"Tillie, just take the flower out of your hair. Put it in your box," I said, but Tillie refused.

I hugged Dia before we walked to the front door, but she dragged her feet like she had more she wanted to say or like she didn't want to go at all. From the porch steps, I could see Mrs. Chang waiting in her car, and we waved at each other. Outside was entirely purple now. The sky had become a wall of purple, something we couldn't see over or through. Standing next to me, Dia had a purply glow to her; the trees and houses and cars were radiating purple. I stared at my hand, skin shimmering the same color as the whole world. I tried to remember what everything had looked like before, but even my memories were slightly purple. Right now, there was nothing but Amplus, and the idea of blue skies was so far away that it felt like we'd always had a violet sky. Like all there was in the world was sadness and death and the end of things.

With binoculars, you could see the little bumps and craters on the surface of the asteroid, like pores on skin. I'd seen lots of asteroid pictures on the internet.

One of Dad's favorite words since he quit his job was the word "perspective." I knew it had two different meanings. One meaning was that things changed depending on the angle and position from which you looked at them. The other meaning of *perspective* was an attitude or feeling toward a thing.

"The day my perspective changed was the day my whole life restarted," Dad liked to say.

I couldn't tell whether it was the first kind of perspective or the second kind; maybe it was both. I'd have to ask him later.

As Amplus had gotten closer, our perspective from Earth had changed so it was all we could see, but I wondered what *we* looked like to the asteroid. Were we bumpy, green and brown and blue, the way the globe in Mr. Gracen's classroom was? Were there asteroidlings on Amplus, calculating the probability that they were going to hit us, the way we were calculating it? Were they as scared of us as we were of them?

I didn't know the answer to a single question, and even worse, no amount of research could tell me.

"Are you sad?" Dia whispered all of a sudden, jolting me out of my thoughts.

She was asking about what I was already thinking about—the end of the world—and it was a pretty simple question.

I could have told her yes. I knew I could have because Dia was my very best friend in the world and we told each other everything, but suddenly it felt so hard to say this one single word. It felt like saying yes would open up a whole volcano of words that I didn't want to say, words that would have to bubble and boil and burn before erupting out of my body. So I said something different.

"If you flip a coin forty-nine times and it always lands on heads, what do you think you'll get if you flip it a fiftieth time?"

I knew Dia was surprised by the change in conversation, but she played along anyway. "Hmm," she said. "Obviously it has to be heads, right?"

I shook my head. "If it's a regular coin, there's still only fifty-fifty chance that you get heads. So you have just as much chance of getting tails as you do of getting heads."

Dia seemed surprised by this, so I explained that the

probability of a past event (getting heads forty-nine times) does not affect the probability of a future event (getting heads or tails the fiftieth time).

The fact that the sun had risen every day I'd been alive didn't mean that it would rise tomorrow.

The fact that everyone I loved had woken up today didn't mean that they would wake up tomorrow.

The fact that so far, for hundreds and thousands of years, a giant asteroid hadn't knocked us out of the sky didn't mean it never would.

Chance, truly, was random. It didn't have to be even or fair.

Statistics told us what could or would *probably* happen in life, but they never told us what definitely would. Statistics could make us feel like we could predict, but really, life just had to happen and then we had to live with it.

Even if it meant the end of the world.

And I was sad about that, and scared, and tired. And the only way I could tell Dia was through probability.

I couldn't tell if she understood.

Dia hugged me and left then, hurrying to her mom's car, and I went back inside Aunt Miriam's house.

Lucas, Tillie, Dad, and Aunt Miriam were all having breakfast.

I decided to take the garment bag Dia had given me

upstairs, where it would be safe from dogs and prying eyes. As I went up the stairs, I ran my hands along the seams of the bag, trying to feel what it was without really feeling what it was. (I *had* promised, and I didn't want to break my promise).

Maybe Dia had made me an outfit for the end of the world after all?

I used to think it was a bad thing how curious I was, but now I thought it was actually a strength. All good scientists wanted to know more about the world. They found questions and tried to answer them. The question of what was in the garment bag was pretty big and distracting, but I put it away in Tillie's closet until tomorrow.

I was coming back down the stairs when the doorbell rang and Aunt Miriam went to answer it. At first, I thought it was Dia, that she had forgotten something and come back, so I hurried down but then I noticed how strange my aunt's voice sounded. It made me stop when I reached the bottom step.

"Now is not a good time," I heard her saying. The other person spoke, insistent and firm. It was a man with a deep voice, a familiar deep voice, and I realized that it was the same man who had come by on Monday. The same man Uncle Steve had turned away two days ago.

He sounded less patient than he had before, a little bit annoyed.

I heard snatches of things he was saying. "Lone witness" and "additional charges," "threats" and "prior antagonization." I didn't even *know* what ant-agoni-zation was.

Then he said our names—Mom's name, Dad's name, mine—and my heart felt like it would fall right out of my chest. How did he know us? What did he want with us?

The person spoke in a low, serious voice. "You know how important this is. They can't hide forever."

Hide. That word hung in the air, and something hit me like a lightning strike. The way Mom had asked Mrs. Sorensen to watch us, the place her and Dad had gone right after Amplus came, the way Aunt Miriam had picked us up from the neighbor and brought us straight here.

We need to all be together, everyone kept saying.

Nobody leaves the house without asking permission, Mom had said.

It hadn't occurred to me that we were hiding from anything other than the asteroid, that giant miniplanet flying through space toward us, and I waited for my aunt to tell this man so.

"Of course," Aunt Miriam said instead. "Please just let us be together right now. Come back tomorrow," she pleaded.

There was a pause before the man agreed.

"Tomorrow," he said.

Tomorrow before the entire world would explode, this strange man would come for us. For me and Mom and Dad. Why?

I heard his car back out of Aunt Miriam's long driveway. I heard her shut the front door. I heard my aunt sniff a few times like she was crying all over again.

My palms were sweaty and I put my hand over my chest, trying to tell my heart to calm down.

Aunt Miriam jumped when she saw me standing at the bottom of the stairs. "Oh, goodness!" she said. "Hi, Kemi."

"Who was that?"

"Nobody. I mean, just a neighbor," she lied, forgetting that I'd met all their neighbors. She put one arm around my shoulder. "Want to help me with some plans for tomorrow? It's going to be a hard day, but I want you kids to feel like you have a say in what happens."

What did she mean that she wanted us to have say in what happens? We were going to be wiped out by an asteroid! And then whatever we became after would be totally up to chance. That was the definition of having no say in what happened.

"Um, can I help you later?" I asked.

Tomorrow felt as close as a shadow. *Too* close.

I didn't know what was happening with Aunt Miriam or the man who kept coming to look for us, but I knew today was extremely important. And I couldn't get distracted.

If I didn't finish the time capsule by tonight, there would be nothing left of my family.

Exploding Hearts

Everybody in aunt miriam's house was awake by now, and it seemed like we all had last-minute plans for the end of the world. Jen and Lucas and Tillie had been put on Operation Clean the House duty. Aunt Miriam was sitting at the dining table, making phone calls that seemed to make her even sadder than normal. I think she was saying goodbye to all the people she knew and would never see again. And Uncle Steve was playing songs on his headphones, nodding along to them and taking notes. He kept asking Aunt Miriam what she thought about *this* song or *that* song. I wondered when we would play the songs he was choosing. Right away when we woke up tomorrow? Or in the afternoon, around the time the asteroid was supposed to hit? I wondered what our last song would be, the last song we would hear before it was all over.

Grandma was in the kitchen, cooking with Mama Johnson from across the street. They were making giant pots of jollof rice and frying ripe plantains. I could smell the sweet, oily scent from all the way upstairs. It was so weird that food could bring people together on all days, even ones with complicated emotions like the apocalypse. But then I thought about it a little harder and I realized something: People ate on good and bad days. They slept, they prayed, they showered, they washed their hair, they laughed and cried and breathed.

How did people keep doing—keep existing—on the hard days?

I didn't know.

I didn't think I ever would.

I took a shower and had breakfast, and then I pulled the shoebox out from under the bed. Apart from Dad, I still needed Grandma's and Tillie's mementos, but I figured I could pack everybody else's.

Before I could even open the box, though, there was a knock on the door.

It was Dad. "Hey, Grit," he said. He looked even worse than he had yesterday, thinner and smaller and older somehow. He was dying right in front of me. I wanted to cry out and put my arms around him to hold him in place.

Don't leave me, I would beg.

The world was going to end without him.

"Did you find your memento?" I asked, because it was the most hopeful thing I could think of to say. The only thing that wasn't bursting into tears and asking if I could go with him to wherever the radiation sickness was taking him.

But Dad surprised me.

"No, but Mom and me and Lo are in our room. The gang's not complete without you."

"I have to finish the—"

"Time capsule," Dad said. "I know.

"But there's no guarantees about what happens next, Grit," Dad said, and I knew without him saying the words out loud that he was telling me that we might not all make it to the end of the world together. He was telling me that he was getting weaker and weaker, fading slowly.

Dad didn't say it in a worried way either, but like it was just a fact, something nobody could change. "It would be nice if we spent some time just the four of us."

I felt a pinch in my chest. No matter what, the world was ending tomorrow. What we left behind was important, but so was spending our last days together.

So I slid the box under Tillie's bottom bunk bed and followed Dad to his and Mom's room. Lo was sitting on the bed next to Mom, holding her stuffie and babbling.

Mom gave me a sad smile as I sat on the bed. "Hi, honey," she said, holding out her hand to me. Her hand felt cold and clammy when I touched it.

It occurred to me now that maybe Mom had the same thing Dad did, that she wasn't just in bed because of the baby and the sadness.

"Are you sick?" I whispered, afraid to know the answer. Everyone else, except Dad, seemed healthy so far, but Mom looked weaker and sadder every day.

"I'm not sick," Mom promised me, and I squeezed her hand.

"I love both of you more than science," I told Mom and Dad. I was just blurting things out today, but I didn't regret it because I needed them to know that I loved them more than anything in the world. Sometimes it might seem like I loved Dad more, but that wasn't true. I loved my parents in different ways, but the same amount.

"I love you more than hot dogs, Grit," Dad said, ruffling my hair.

But Mom just said, tears in her eyes, "I know."

"I think," Dad said, sitting on the edge of the bed next to Mom, "we should have a sing-off."

"Yeah, let's have a sing-off!" I said.

Mom made a face and loud-whispered to Lo, as Dad

rigged his phone up to a speaker, "Why do the worst singers always suggest the sing-offs?"

I giggled, and we listened as Dad did the most terrible rendition of "It's My Life." It was terrible not just because he was off-beat and off-key but because he coughed quite a bit through it too. We all tried to ignore the elephant of him dying slowly right here in front of us. We were trying to be thankful that we had this time to be together, even if all of this would end soon.

It was my turn next and I sang a just-as-terrible version of "We Are the Champions." Lo seemed to know what we were doing because she started her own off-key version of sing-yelling and clapping her hands so Dad put on "The Wheels on the Bus," and we let her just shout for four minutes. By the end of it, my ears were sore, but Lo looked so pleased with herself.

Mom was the best singer out of all of us. When it was her turn, she looked too sad and I thought she'd shake her head and ask me or Dad to take her turn. (I shuddered at the thought of Lo getting another turn.) But instead she picked up her phone like it was a microphone, and right there in her bed, hand on her belly, she did the most amazing version of "I Will Always Love You." I felt like crying from how clear her voice was; I felt like crying because it seemed like, in a way, we were saying goodbye. That we'd spent every day since Amplus came saying goodbye to each other. Saying goodbye to each other and Grandma and my uncles and my aunt and my cousins.

I wondered how I could ever put the things I really wanted to save in a time capsule.

I wanted the next earthlings to know the way Dad's eyes got crinkly when he smiled, the way Grandma had a gap between her teeth, the way the bracelets Jen wore made her hands look long and elegant, the fact that Z was a dancer before she was even born. I wanted them to know how Mom was the most talented person I'd ever met. She was someone who could do so many things, like sing and dance and make art and do research and teach. I wanted them to know someday that Uncle Steve wore sweater vests and that Aunt Miriam cried when she laughed too hard, that Lucas was the pickiest eater ever and that Tillie always sat by me whenever she could and that, on our last day, my heart was so full of all these people I loved that it felt like bursting. It felt like it could split open like a pair of too-tight jeans and spill out onto the guest room floor of Aunt Miriam's house.

Was it bad when your heart felt like exploding? *Probably,* I thought, but I couldn't think of any exact statistics off the top of my head.

I wondered what that would look like—if my heart spilled onto the guest room floor.

I knew it would be blood and guts and arteries and veins, but it would also be songs and numbers, percentages and good food, happiness and loneliness and so many other things. It would be good things and bad things, sweet things and bitter things, things that last forever and things that only last a moment. It would be big enough to fit every feeling in the world, and the asteroid wouldn't be able to touch it.

Mom and Dad and Lo and I spent most of the afternoon together. We included Z too by talking to her and touching Mom's belly, feeling her pirouettes and twirls. I had the idea for us to build a fort with the sheets on Mom and Dad's bed, and Dad invented a not-scary scary story, using his phone as a flashlight. (I obviously knew the statistical probability that ghosts exist was very small, which was what made it not-scary.) Lo tried to chew on the ends of my braids for most of the story, but she liked shouting "fort fort!" Mom fell asleep during our fort games, and Dad was getting tired too, so I snuck out of the room with Lo so they could rest.

I took Lo to the kitchen and left her with Grandma, but I got my empty shoebox from Tillie's room and went out to the backyard. Tillie was immediately on my heels. "What are you doing? Can I come?"

"I'm going to find the perfect spot for the time capsule," I told her. "Do you want to bury your miscellaneous things box too so it's safe?"

Tillie shook her head. "I want to keep it," she said.

I didn't think she understood that you couldn't *keep* anything when you were dead, but maybe it was okay. Maybe it was fine just to have the things she loved with her when the asteroid hit.

We went into Aunt Miriam's garden shed and pulled out shovels we could use to dig up the ground and then we walked around looking for the best place in the garden to put the box. I was only going to find the right spot for it; I wasn't going to put it in yet.

I tried not to look at Amplus, but the entire horizon *was* Amplus. Purple, shiny, and honestly? More sad than happy. I had been trying to focus on being hopeful, but the answer to the question Dia had asked was this: I *was* sad. The end meant new beginnings, but it also meant the ending of things I loved so, so much. And it made me want to curl up in a ball and cry.

Tillie and I found what looked like a good spot next to Aunt Miriam's tomatoes and were just starting to make a hole with our shovels when we heard a loud noise and Lucas and Jasper, Mama Johnson's grandson, came running through the gate.

They were spraying each other with water guns. I stood frozen as Jasper ran by us, squirting a stream of water that landed all over the front of my sweater and on the box.

I burst into tears.

Was it because of the boys or because I was already supersad about the end of the world?

I didn't know, and it didn't matter.

Lucas came running over right away. "Jasper, *stop!*" He put a hand on my shoulder. "We were just playing around."

"Is it wet?" Tillie asked, looking at the box.

I dropped the shovel and hurried inside, hugging the shoebox to my chest. I heard Tillie running after me and Lucas calling my name, but I didn't stop.

Not until I was upstairs in the bathroom, the shoebox still cradled to my chest.

I probably wet the cardboard even more with my tears.

I didn't stop until I heard Aunt Miriam knocking on the bathroom door. "Kemi," she said. "Honey, are you okay? Can you open up for me?"

I wiped my face on my shirt, then opened the door.

My aunt was standing there with an expression on her face that I couldn't read.

Lucas was behind her, staring down at the ground.

"I'm sorry, Kemi," he mumbled, like he was too ashamed to look at me.

"It's okay," I said over the lump in my throat.

"Lucas promises to be more sensitive in the future.

Don't you, Luc?" Aunt Miriam asked, and he nodded.

Aunt Miriam turned and left, and Lucas shoved his hands in his pocket, still not looking at me. "I guess I'm banned from helping with the time capsule now," he said, sounding glum.

I was pretty mad at Lucas and feeling a bunch of other things I couldn't say out loud, but I knew he was sorry and he *had* been a big help so far with the time capsule, so I said, "Want to help me pack it?"

The Spectaculars

LUCAS AND TILLIE WATCHED ME AS I LAID OUT ALL THE items everyone had given me plus the items we had brought from my house on the carpet of her room. There were the pair of fuzzy dark blue house slippers that Mom believed was hers and that Dad swore was his. This meant that if Dad couldn't find "his" shoes, Mom was wearing them. And the other way around. But I think they secretly liked sharing the shoes because one time when I suggested Dad get Mom a new pair for Christmas, so they could finally stop fighting, he laughed and said, "Now why would I do a thing like that?"

There was the framed picture of us dressed as superheroes.

It was from the Halloween before Lo was born so Mom's belly was even rounder and fuller in the pictures than it was now with Baby Z. She was dressed in red and blue like Superwoman. Dad was dressed like Iron Man in shiny red armor and I was in all black like Black Panther.

It was our first October living in Pineview, and even though I was getting kind of old for trick-or-treating, I had been so excited about doing it in our new neighborhood. All our neighbors' houses had fancy lights and pumpkins and wreaths, so I thought they'd also give out great treats. But almost as soon as we left our house, other trick-or-treaters gave us weird looks and some people shut off their lights before we reached their front door. After this had happened a few times and only Mrs. Sorensen had opened her door for us, Dad suggested we go and get ice cream. My heart was heavy, like a stone in my chest, and I felt like crying the whole time we were at Galileo's Ice Cream Parlor. When we got back home to our house that was still full of boxes and things we hadn't unpacked, Mom brought out a giant bag of candy and Dad said, "You know what I think we're missing with our costumes, Grit? Backstories."

I was still feeling pretty sad, so tugging at my black leggings, I said, "I just want to take this off."

"You know, honey, people aren't always good or kind or fair," he said, "but that doesn't change what we are."

I sighed, not in the mood to talk. "What are we?"

I thought he'd say Black or humans or something, but he said, "Superheroes!" And ran around the room pretending to fly with one arm up like Superman.

I couldn't help giggling a little. "You're Iron Man. You fly with a *jet suit*," I pointed out.

"What, you mean I can't climb things with a spidery web?" He tried to shoot rope out of his hands.

I sighed again. When Dad wasn't working, he was always the goofiest of all three of us. "You're not Spider-Man, Dad."

"What about a giant hammer? Surely, I have one of those."

"That's Thor!" Mom said, joining in and laughing. She was sitting on the couch with her feet raised on the ottoman. Her feet had gotten swollen a lot close to when Lo was born.

"Well, that's just it, isn't it? I don't know what our backstories are. Forget our costumes—let's come up with our own superheroes."

Reluctantly, I sat down on the couch next to Mom.

"Grab your notebook, Grit," Dad said. "This is going to be good."

My notebook was on the dining table, so I got it and a pen and sat back down.

Our own superheroes, I wrote at the top of a new page in my notebook.

Dad paced the living room. "With Baby, there're four of us, so we can be the Fantastic Four."

"That already exists," I said.

"The Final Four."

"That sounds ominous," Mom said, and I nodded in agreement even though I wasn't sure what ominous meant. (I wrote it down in my notebook and researched it later. Ominous: "threatening" or "unfavorable.")

"The Incredibles," Dad suggested.

Mom and I looked at each and burst into laughter. Mom said, "Jared, you're doing this on purpose, aren't you?"

"Oh, I'm sorry!" Dad joked. "Am I supposed to be an expert on superhero backstories?"

"Any ideas, Kem?" Mom asked.

I bit my lip and thought about it.

"How about the Spectaculars?" I said.

"The Spectaculars," Mom repeated, a twinkle in her eye.

"The Spectaculars!" Dad said, like it was the best superhero name he'd ever heard.

"What are our powers?"

Mine was being good at statistics, so we called me "Stat-girl." Dad said his superpower was sleeping, so his name was "The Sleep Bandit." Mom's super-special power was obviously art, so we simply called her "*Collage*." (I made a special note in my notebook that you had to say it like that, in kind of a deep, mysterious, and superhero-y voice. Not Collage, but *Collage*.) Mom said that Lo's superpower was kicking her in the ribs, so Dad acted like he'd had a brilliant idea, a *vision* even.

"Karate Kid," he said, drawing out the words dramatically.

"Quick Kick," Mom said, and we went with that one instead.

Once we had our superhero names, it was time to make superhero cards. So Dad took pictures of each of us, and one of all three (or four) of us.

Later, I heard Mom and Dad talking in low voices downstairs while I was supposed to be upstairs getting ready for bed.

"Maybe this move was a bad idea," Mom said, and I could imagine her rubbing her temple the way she did when she was stressed or frustrated. "How are we going to raise two daughters in a neighborhood like this? What century are we in? What *world* are we in?"

I knew she meant that she was surprised the people in

Pineview were still so unwelcoming to Black people in 2023. In 2023, when we had Martin Luther King Jr. Day and had a former Black president and a Black woman vice president. We had laws that meant Black and brown people didn't have to stand on buses anymore.

"I don't think they hate us," Dad said. "They just don't believe we belong here, in their neighborhood, with their 'good' schools and nice houses and expensive cars."

"That feels a lot like hate to me," Mom said.

"So what do we do?" Dad asked. "What are the possibilities?"

"We move," Mom said. "We make a fuss. We act just as awful to them as they've been to us."

"*Or?*" Dad said.

Mom sighed. "Or we stay put and know that we belong here too."

That was what we had done. Stayed put and known in our hearts that we belonged in Pineview.

Because we were the Spectaculars.

Now, I put the picture of the three of us in the shoebox with the menu.

"What's that?" Lucas asked as I quickly stuffed the forever T-shirt into the box without letting him see it.

"Just a shirt," I said.

Next was another framed picture, one of my whole

family. Grandma, Uncle Steve, Aunt Miriam, Jen, Lucas, Tillie, Skip, me, Mom, Dad, Uncle Jeremiah, and Lo. It was taken one Sunday, three months ago, after church in Aunt Miriam's backyard when Mom and Dad knew she was pregnant but hadn't told anyone. So Baby Z was technically in it too, just like Lo had been in the pictures of us as The Spectaculars. I knew these were the things Mom meant when she'd said "everything" and "pictures, books, clothes, things we made, things we bought."

I put an old copy of *Where The Wild Things Are* in the shoebox because it was one of me and Mom's favorite books to read together. I loved the book with all my heart. It was about the way imagining something could make it true, about the way home was the place where you were loved the most. This specific book was about home, but whenever she changed the names of characters in books, Mom got me to go to the furthest places and to have wild adventures. She put me in Rapunzel's castle and Cinderella's cellar and Max's room in *Where The Wild Things Are*.

I found Lo's stuffie downstairs and put it in the time capsule. That was her memento.

"I have mine," Tillie said, handing me a folded piece of paper.

It was a letter, and all it said was: *I love you, Tillie.*

"Um," I said. I was seriously wondering if Tillie even

understood the purpose of the time capsule. What would the next earthlings do with a note?

"Good job, Till Pickle," Lucas said, being nice to his sister for once.

So then I had no choice but to say, "Yeah, good job, Tillie."

I put the note in the box, even though the next earthlings would probably wonder why a past earthling had written them a love letter.

I put in the smallest one of Mom's Color Me vases—it was orange and white and green—and I was a little worried it would break, so I wrapped the forever T-shirt around it. I put in my old doll, Ella. Ella had long brown hair and she used to be my favorite, just the way Blue was Lo's favorite. When I was little, I kept losing Ella and I'd get really upset about it. Luckily, Dad was an expert at finding her; he always seemed to know exactly where she was. One day, I woke up in the middle of the night and snuck into Mom and Dad's room because I was scared of the storm. And Dad was sitting in bed, braiding Ella's hair! Every time Ella went missing, it was because Dad had taken her and was practicing how to braid her hair so he could braid mine.

"Jen showed me how," Dad admitted, looking a little embarrassed but smiling from ear to ear. "That girl is so talented. I'm going to be first in line at her salon one day."

Now, all these years later, Dad still couldn't do corn-rows or anything like Jen could, but he could give me two mostly even plaits on either side of my head.

I put in some of Mom's paintbrushes and one of my old notebooks full of facts and science. I put in one of Skip's collars and an old butterfly clip Dia had given me from her '90s phase last year and Lucas's Unique and Uncle Steve and Aunt Miriam's socks and plaque, Jen's neon open sign, and one of Grandma's recipe books that she'd said I could have.

Then I stared at the box that was so, so full by now. Anything else I put in would have to be super small. Dad's memento would have to be super small now.

I frowned.

"What's wrong?" Lucas asked.

"I think . . . I think the time capsule is done," I said. "Except for Dad's thing."

"That's great, Neurokemical!" Lucas said. "Why do you look like someone kicked your kemileon?"

I didn't say anything about Lucas's pun.

I didn't know *what* to say, because it wasn't enough. Where was the way Dad knew how every movie would end or the way Mom was a zombie before she had her morning coffee or the way Lo looked dressed like a bunny last Hal-loween? Where was *I*? Where were all the things I loved and hated and wanted?

"There's something missing," I said. "Something that isn't Dad's memento."

"Maybe we need more pictures or something? You could take some with my cell phone," Lucas offered. I think he still felt bad about before and the water squirting.

More photos *would* be nice, but I didn't think they could capture all the tangly feelings in my chest. The wanting to be twelve but being afraid of being older than eleven; the special ways Lo annoyed me and the special ways I loved her as her older sister.

More pictures wouldn't—couldn't—capture all the things I would miss.

It couldn't capture all the things I wouldn't miss either.

So I wrote some lists and added them to the box.

THINGS I WILL MISS

The way the sun feels on my face in the summer

Putting on warm clothes from the dryer

Sand between my toes

My family

Slurpees

Lo's belly laughs

Dad's hugs

Shoebox hauls with Mom

Climbing trees

Skip always looking happy to see me

Stuffies

Lucas sleeping with a stuffie

Naps

Superfast Wi-Fi

The smell of the air after it has rained

Jollof rice

The first snowfall

New braids

Piper Peters saying "I'm not going down without a fight"

Shooting stars

My room

Music

Dogs that look like their human

Humans that look like their dog

When it's so cold I can see my breath

Math

Pizza with extra cheese

THINGS I WON'T MISS

When you can't finish your ice cream in time and it
drips in between your fingers

Flossing

Wedgies

Bad breath

Bedtime

That pulling feeling when I'm getting my hair
braided

Custard

Snot icicles in winter

Things that are too spicy

Things that are too hot

Bird poop

The skin on top of warm milk

Storms

Tomato soup

Worms

Star Clusters

I BOLTED UPRIGHT IN THE MIDDLE OF THE NIGHT (AND knocked my head on Tillie's bed) because I had an idea. I was pretty sure—I was confident, even—that I'd solved the mystery of what Dad's memento should be.

"Can I go where you're going?" Tillie murmured, still mostly asleep.

"I'll be right back," I promised her.

I tiptoed out of the room, into the hallway, and over to Mom and Dad's room. I didn't want to wake Mom, but I really had to talk to Dad.

I knocked once on their door.

Then I stuck my head in the doorway and whispered for Dad.

He yawned. "Kemi, is that you?"

"Yeah," I said. "Can you talk for a minute?"

Dad coughed, then slowly slid out of the left side of the bed. He moved like a million things inside him were aching, like his bones were crumbling.

I bit my lip.

Mom was fast asleep, so we shut the door and stood in the hallway.

"I think I solved it," I told Dad. "I know what your memento should be!"

Dad looked surprised. "Really?" He coughed again.

I nodded. "It's outside, though. Can you . . . can you make it there?"

"Don't worry about me," Dad said with a wink, still moving like he was even older than Grandma.

We went slowly down the stairs, put on our shoes, and slipped out the front door. When we got outside and I looked up at the sky, I was . . . disappointed.

It was all just purple, like someone had pulled a cloth over the entire sky.

"I forgot about Amplus," I told Dad, feeling embarrassed. "I mean, I didn't *forget* about it but about the way it's blocking the sky. I wanted you to see the stars."

"I see the stars," Dad said, sitting down on the front porch steps and looking up at the sky. He coughed so hard now I thought his chest might explode.

"Do you need anything?" I asked, trying not to show how scared I was. "Water?"

Dad shook his head and pointed up. "The stars are hard to see but they're there. Always."

I sat down next to Dad, squinting. I couldn't see anything but inky purple. We were going to die in this purple. For the first time, I imagined Amplus like a gas, something that would spread over us and cover us and suffocate us the way it had done with the sky.

"Look closely, Grit," Dad said, his shaky hand still stretched upward. At first, I couldn't see what he was pointing at. It all looked the same to me. Uniformly purple.

But then.

Then I saw the slightest twinkle. It was a bit of orange, a pinprick of light.

I gasped and clapped my hands.

"Oh my gosh! I see it!" I exclaimed.

Dad laughed. "It's the things that are hardest to see that are worth looking for," he said, leaning back on his hands. He looked really happy and peaceful, even with the glow of purple radiating off him. Even though his skin looked paper-thin and his voice was hoarse from all the coughing.

"I remembered about when you were younger, how your dad gave you the stargazing kit with the mini-telescope?" I said, explaining why I had added this to the experiment of finding the thing Dad loved. "I remembered how when I was little, you'd take me outside on your shoulders and point out the stars to me."

It was because Dad loved stars that he'd suggested putting them on the ceiling of my bedroom years ago.

But Dad had gotten so busy that we hadn't looked at the stars together in years. "When my father gave me the stargazing kit, he told me that when you look at the stars, you're literally looking at the past. Do you know why that is?" Dad asked.

I shook my head.

"It's because their light takes millions of years to reach Earth," Dad said. "When you think about it, that means the past is always out there somewhere, still existing. When I lost my dad in college, that thought brought me so much comfort. The stars remind me that we never really lose things or people we love; they are just closer or farther away."

Dad's words reminded me of Fact Four from my research about the end of the world: matter can change from one form to another, but it can never be created or destroyed. The end of something—even a human, even a planet—is just a change.

Somehow, that made The End seem less scary and final and more like science, a chemical reaction or a math equation. We couldn't change it, but it couldn't destroy us.

"There's another one," Dad said, pointing out another star, and just like magic, I started to see them all. The stars behind Amplus. The stars Amplus couldn't hide.

I remembered the thing I'd decided to look up but never had: were stars bigger than asteroids?

I asked the question out loud and Dad said, "I actually don't know the answer to that. I'm so rusty on all my astronomy."

"That's okay," I said, and made a mental note not to forget to check this later, if I had time.

"Do you know what else I love about stars? I like this idea of us, humans, being like stars in the sky. I like the idea that people absorb and emit energy just the way stars do. We put out light and we receive it too," he said, scratching his chin. He coughed once, then cleared his throat. "Then we surround ourselves with the stars that know and love us, making our very own star clusters. It's not a perfect analogy, but it's one I've always liked."

"Dad," I said, in a fake whisper like I was telling a shocking secret, "I think this means you like science."

Dad smiled, but the truth of it *was* shocking.

I'd always thought I loved science since the first day I started learning about it, in kindergarten. But actually, it turned out, it was yet another thing I inherited from Dad. Like rolling my tongue or loving home renovation shows.

We watched the stars for a bit longer, and then we went to bed for the very last time.

It was only when I was snuggled up under the covers, drifting to sleep that I realized something: Dad said he loved the stars, but he hadn't said they were the thing he loved *most* in the world.

I hadn't found his memento after all.

ZERO DAYS
Until the End of the World

The End of
the End of
the World

I GUESS I PLANNED TO SLEEP THROUGH THE END OF THE world.

It wasn't just that I'd been up till past midnight with Dad, looking at the stars.

It was that my body made an executive decision that it did not want to eat jollof rice or have a last song or watch the asteroid blast everybody I loved to bits. An executive decision is a decision the person in charge makes, like when Piper Peters ordered the painters to have the windows done on time *or else*.

I think I would have gotten away with it too.

I could have slept through the end of the world.

Except for Grandma.

Grandma was shaking me awake at nine o'clock sharp, saying, "Kemi, you need to get up."

I groaned.

"Kemi," she said so softly her words were almost a breath. "I have something for your box."

I sat up, rubbing the sleep from my eyes. "You do?"

She was holding a small container, the kind you use for leftovers. But instead of leftovers, there were brownish sticks inside.

"Kuli kuli," she said. "Do you want one?"

She opened the container and I dipped in, chomping down hard on the snack. The stick was so hard, I knew that if I didn't break it, it would break my tooth. I'd had kuli kuli lots of times before because it was Dad's favorite and, whenever Grandma brought some over for us, Mom and I had to hide it away so Dad didn't eat it all.

"Thank you," I said. It tasted peanuty and dry and a little bit spicy.

Of course, Grandma had made something for the next earthlings. Love in the form of a snack.

I was still chewing when Grandma gently touched my arm and said, "It's time . . ."

And then I remembered why we needed an end-of-the-world time capsule to begin with. "For the asteroid?" I asked, my voice a whisper. I couldn't believe I'd forgotten about Amplus for even a second.

Grandma gave me a sad look and shook her head. "First, there's someone here for you."

FOUR HOURS
Until the End of the World

How to Bury a Time Capsule

THE MAN SAT IN AUNT MIRIAM'S LIVING ROOM. I COULD
see him over the railing of the landing. He was bald, with a
shiny head that the light bounced off of. The lights were on
in the living room because there was no sunshine pouring
in from the opened blinds. I had seen from Tillie's window
that the sky was no longer purple like it had been last night.
It was black.

I stayed in the landing, staring at the man from above.
He flexed and unflexed his hands, like maybe he'd been in
a fight recently. He looked stern and serious.

He was here *for me*. Not me and Mom and Dad, but me.

231

I just knew he was the same man who had kept bothering us since we came to Aunt Miriam's.

In the kitchen and the dining room, there was a bustle like the sound an engine makes, low and urgent, steady like a heartbeat. All the grown-ups were down there getting ready for the asteroid. I thought I could hear Uncle Jeremiah, and I was pretty sure that was Mom's friend Susan's singsong voice.

I tiptoed down the hall to Lucas's room.

He was on his bed, playing on his phone with Skip by his side.

Skip bolted over to me and started jumping on me. I wanted to bend down and pet him, but I knew doing that would take up more time than I had.

So even though I desperately wanted to say hi to him, I whispered, "Not now, Skip." He kept hovering around me, begging to give me dog kisses, but I forced myself to ignore him.

"Lucas, we have to go and bury it," I told him in an urgent voice.

"Bury it?" he said.

"The time capsule," I said, a little bit impatient.

"But your dad's . . ."

"We don't have time for his memento anymore." It was the saddest thing, but it was true. We were out of time. If I didn't bury the time capsule now, I wouldn't have time to and there would be nothing at all for the next earthlings to know us by.

Lucas didn't say anything, so I said, "You have to help me. There's someone downstairs waiting for me. You need to distract him so I can sneak into the yard, and then we'll bury it."

"How am I supposed to distract him?" Lucas looked like I'd suggested he wear his head on his toe.

"I don't know! Be yourself," I said, because it seemed like the kind of advice people gave all the time.

Lucas sighed. "Gee, thanks," he said.

"So will you do it?" I asked, so hopeful my chest felt like it might burst.

Lucas hesitated for a minute, but then he said, "Okay."

He stood up and stuck his phone in the pocket of his suit. *Lucas was wearing a suit!* It was black with a white collared shirt underneath. He looked older and less like my troublemaking cousin. I realized he was staring at me too.

"You're not going to change?" he asked.

I was in my pajamas, the gray ones with the white sheep on them.

"Why would I?" I shrugged.

"Because it's almost time," Lucas said. "For the—"

But I was already turning and leaving his room. I went

to Tillie's room to get the time capsule. Like she had some kind of radar for when Lucas and I were about to have an adventure, Tillie appeared in the doorway. The yellow flower was in her hair again, but this time it looked lifeless and almost brown. I knew she wouldn't take it out even if I asked, so I didn't.

"Is it happening now?" Tillie asked.

"Yes," I said simply, and her eyes widened.

Lucas had gone downstairs ahead of us, and I heard him now attempting to make small talk with the man.

"Do you, er, have a cell phone?" Lucas asked, and I cringed. He was doing a horrible job of distracting the stranger.

"I do," the man said. He seemed extremely bored, and I swear I saw him glance toward the stairs.

"Have you heard of the video game *Finite*?" Lucas tried again.

"I have not," the man said, still sounding like Lucas was torturing him.

"It's so good. It's even better if you believe in aliens," Lucas said, his voice getting kind of excited.

"Aliens?" the man repeated.

Tillie and I crept down, one step at a time.

Then while Lucas explained the game to the man, Tillie and I made a run for the back door, careful so no one saw us.

After all the trouble we'd gone through to put together the time capsule, I couldn't risk not getting a chance to bury it.

The sliding door that led out back sounded so loud opening that I was sure we'd been caught, but there was too much commotion happening around the house. The grown-ups were all making or serving food, and Lucas was still with the man.

I breathed a huge sigh of relief as we got outside. Almost immediately, though, I froze.

In addition to the black sky, a strong wind was blowing through the air, making it dusty and hard to see.

I took a deep breath and marched toward the shed, grabbed three shovels, and hurried toward the spot in the garden I'd chosen yesterday, next to Aunt Miriam's tomatoes.

"Here," I said, handing Tillie the smallest shovel.

It still looked way too big in her hand.

Lucas joined us a minute later. "I put on a game show for him," he said. Then he added, "Maybe we shouldn't do this!"

"We're going to have to dig as fast as we can," I told them both, ignoring him. The wind was howling now, so I had to practically shout to be heard over it. "No stopping until we're done."

I pushed my shovel into the ground and Lucas did the same.

Digging was more difficult than I thought it would be. The earth didn't just turn over the way I expected. Instead, it felt a bit like I was hitting rock.

I wondered if Tillie had the right idea after all—to *keep* the things that mattered, not try to hide them.

I kept shoveling.

"This is hard!" Tillie shouted.

"Keep going!" I said, even as something blew into my eye. I blinked several times in a row but didn't stop.

You're doing this so your family is not forgotten, I told myself. *You have to keep going.*

Tillie sneezed.

And then the first raindrop landed on my nose.

"Maybe we should stop," Lucas said, but he wasn't asking. He was already leaning against his shovel and panting.

"No!" I shouted.

More raindrops.

I kept digging.

"Kemi!" someone said.

I kept digging and digging and digging, and I thought of how Amplus was creeping closer every minute, how it was only a handful of hours until it knocked us right out of the sky. How had I thought that was anything but sad? How had I thought that was anything but final?

The rain started falling faster on my head.

I swore under my breath, but I didn't stop. I couldn't stop.

There wasn't enough time.

The asteroid was about to hit and we were all about to die and this was the only chance we had of being remembered.

"Kemi!"

There was finally a big enough hole, so I dropped the time capsule in and started using my hands to cover it with soil. I was on my knees, burying it as the rain started to come down hard against my skin.

"That's enough," someone said, putting a hand on my shoulder.

"I'm not finished!" I shouted and kept burying, my palms covered in mud.

"Kemi!"

"I'm. Not. Finished!" I yelled, but it wasn't Lucas who was calling my name. It was Uncle Steve. He picked me up from behind as I tried to fight and kick and scream. The time capsule was only half-covered.

It was only half-covered and Amplus and the next earthlings and—

"Enough," Uncle Steve said, as he carried me into the house.

"Enough."

THREE HOURS
Until the End of the World

Failure

UNCLE STEVE PUT ME DOWN ON THE COUCH AND Grandma covered me in a blanket, while the man watched.

I heard Aunt Miriam getting mad at Lucas.

"It's almost time to go, and you're helping her sneak into the backyard?" she asked.

I heard Lucas answering, his voice quiet. "I was trying to help."

"It was an adventure," Tillie said, and she sounded like she was crying.

I thought of the time capsule, only half-buried, exposed to the rain. Exposed to the asteroid.

We were going to be forgotten. The asteroid was going to hit and it was going to destroy us and I hadn't managed to save a single thing to remember us by.

"Kemi," Aunt Miriam said, coming to kneel in front of me. She pointed at the man on the other couch across from me. "This is Officer Wentzel. He wants to talk to you because you saw some things other people didn't. There was a parking lot incident, right? Officer Wentzel has already talked to your mom."

I couldn't look at him, couldn't look at his shiny head or his steady green eyes or the notepad.

Luckily, I didn't have to.

Dad entered the room and came and sat in the seat beside me. He looked the sickest I'd ever seen him. His skin was almost see-through. But when he took my hand, I felt less afraid.

"It's okay, Grit," he said.

The air was ice-cold.

"I need my coat," I whispered.

"I'll get it," Jen offered, disappearing and coming back a few seconds later with my puffy coat. I wore it and then draped the blanket over myself again.

I still felt cold.

Aunt Miriam asked everyone to leave the living room.

She pulled over a chair from the dining table and sat on my other side. "I'm here," she whispered.

"Kemi," Officer Wentzel said. "I want you to talk to me, okay? We spoke to your mother days ago, but now it's your turn. I need you to tell me about the morning your father was murdered."

Part II

How the Sun Burned Out

WE FIRST NOTICED SOMETHING WAS WRONG BECAUSE OF Lo.

It was a Sunday morning in April, and the three of us—me, Mom, and Dad—were sitting at the dining table, discussing a news story Dad was reading on his tablet.

Dad made pancakes; Mom and I set the table.

We had the television low in the background, and Mom let Lo wriggle off her lap while we ate.

"Cirque du Soleil is in town next month!" Dad said as he read through the Arts part of the paper.

But Lo was especially restless that morning, screaming, "NOMMY! NOMMY!" and running around the living room.

Sighing, Dad walked over to where Lo was standing and picked her up.

"No, we *don't* eat the tele—" As Dad picked her up, his voice stopped abruptly. We heard a loud sound, a horrible sound.

"Bim?" Dad said Mom's name like he was a little bit breathless; something had knocked the wind right out of him.

As Mom and I ran over to him, Dad crumpled to the ground, Lo slipping out from his arms. There were shouts and loud footsteps as someone ran out of our house. Someone had *been* inside our house. They had entered through our front door while we were eating, and when Dad had walked into the living room to pick up Lo, they had shot at him. Lo immediately started wailing. Dad was on his back, his eyes wide-open, staring like he was looking over at the television. Like there was something there he'd never seen before, something he'd never imagined.

I didn't know how I got onto the ground beside him, but I was kneeling, trying to shake him awake even as I saw it. Bright red. It spread across his chest like Mom's paint dyeing a canvas.

Bim?

It had sounded like a question.

Dad's final word.

Famous Last Word

SCIENTISTS BELIEVE THAT, STATISTICALLY, THE MOST common last word is "love." But that's usually when people are expecting to die. Like when they're sick or elderly or being executed.

If you don't expect to die, though, sometimes you are cut off midsentence.

"Get me my—"

"I think I have a—"

"My head—"

You can be cut off mid-action too. Picking your nose, doing a left turn in your car, or reaching for something in your purse.

Before Sunday, I'd never seen someone die before.

I don't know what Dad's final thought was.

Maybe it was something ordinary, like, *This carpet is soft*.

Maybe it was something big, like about all the people he loved.

Maybe it was something awful, like about how much being shot hurt.

Or maybe he thought about how he'd never found the thing he loved most, the thing he quit his job for.

I think, when I die, when the asteroid hits, I will be thinking of numbers, of facts and probability.

If he had found what he loved, Dad might have been thinking about that too.

If he had found his passion, Dad might have said, "Grab me my paintbrush" or "Run that marathon for me" or something that would tell us about what mattered to him and how he wanted to be remembered. Something that told us what he wanted the world to be like without him.

Now I hug the blanket tighter around myself.

"What else do you remember?" Aunt Miriam asks in a soft feelings-doctor voice.

The air is so cold, I half expect icicles to start sprouting from my eyelashes, from my nostrils. I expect my breath to start forming clouds. The only thing that helps is Dad's hand, warm and steady in mine. I move closer to him so our thighs are touching.

Dad has always been the person that makes me feel safe.

The last time I remember being afraid, really afraid, was when we saw Mr. Vance at the parking lot of Pineview's Grab 'N Pay last month. Our cars were both backing up at the same time and his SUV had rammed into the back of our Honda. Mr. Vance said a whole string of curse words as he got out of his car.

Dad opened his door and stepped out too.

"What are you, blind? You didn't see my car?" Mr. Vance asked.

"You rammed into *me*," Dad said.

"That's not possible," Mr. Vance bellowed. He tugged at his three-coin necklace like it was too tight around his neck. "I'm going to call the police."

"Call them," Dad said.

They argued for a few more minutes before Mrs. Vance got out of the passenger seat. She had a blond bob and dark red lipstick. "Harry, please let's go," she said, walking to the front of the car where Dad and Mr. Vance stood.

"June, wait in the car!" Mr. Vance yelled.

"Harry, come on," she said, grabbing his elbow.

He jerked his arm so hard that she stumbled backward into the front of the car.

Dad stepped closer toward Mr. Vance, while Mrs. Vance straightened her skirt.

"Let's go," she said one last time, and finally Mr. Vance backed away from Dad and started to get in his car.

"You people don't belong here," he spat. "This is our side of Elderton. Go back to yours." He said some other stuff to Dad, stuff that made me shiver. Then Mr. Vance got into his car and slammed his door before he drove away.

Dad watched them go, his shoulders hunched until they disappeared around the bend. His back was to me, but it didn't matter. I knew his eyes were sad, and maybe just a little scared, like mine.

Dad sighed as he entered the car and shut the door.

He gave me a too-bright smile. "Ready to go? Let's get that ice cream home before it melts."

I sat on my hands to keep them from shaking. My eyes stung the way they did before they welled up with tears. I fought them back all the way past the roundabout that led to our street. All our houses sat side by side, looking so similar but somehow we were still different. Mr. Vance's car was parked in the driveway of the house beside ours already, the back was dented, a brand-new dimple in the metal. I could see a bit of silver paint on his black SUV from our car, but luckily there was no one in Mr. Vance's driveway.

"Why do they hate us so much?"

Dad was silent a minute. It was when we'd pulled up

into our driveway and he'd stopped the car that he said, "Some people prefer to do what is easy, Grit, and hate is easy. Anger is easy."

"Maybe we should move back to the north side," I said.

Dad nodded. "That's certainly an option," he said, hands resting on the steering wheel. "As you grow up, you're going to hear a lot of opinions about the right way to be Black. A lot of people will tell you to turn the other cheek or stay in your lane or just be quiet, stay in the neighborhood where everyone looks like you. But you deserve a world where the way you're treated is based on your character and not your skin color. And you're allowed to fight for that world; you're allowed to make waves.

"Making waves doesn't always mean protesting, though it can. It also means being you, unapologetically you. Living and making friends and going to school and taking up space in the world. As Black people, sometimes that's the loudest statement we can make. Saying, we are here and we matter."

"Wouldn't we matter just as much on the north side?" I knew it would be sad to leave Pineview Elementary, to leave Dia and Mr. Gracen and all the things I'd gotten used to the last year, but at least we wouldn't have to deal with people like Mr. Vance anymore.

Dad rubbed hard at his eyes. "If I'm being honest with you, Grit, I'm tired. I'm tired of the way we've been treated in Pineview. I'm tired of the odd looks and the suspicion and the disrespect. I'm even more tired of turning on the news and seeing the way Black people are treated everywhere. I'm tired of making a political statement just by existing, just by being Black. And I think that's okay. Tired is okay. I don't have to Make A Statement every minute of every day. I can love myself and love my family and be a human and that's enough.

"Your mom and I made the decision to stay in Pineview, but it would be okay if we decided not to as well. Pineview is no better than anywhere else in Elderton just because it's full of white people. But we moved here to be closer to your mom's work. We moved here because we found a house we loved, and we wanted you girls to know that it's okay to take risks."

I bit my lip because I still wasn't sure, because I was scared.

Dad reached across the console and squeezed my hand. "We're going to be just fine, Grit."

Now, a month later, as I tell Officer Wentzel about that day, Dad squeezes my hand again on Aunt Miriam's couch, but I don't squeeze back.

"You said everything was going to be fine," I say, and there is something hot in my voice, something like anger. "How is it fine if you're dead?"

"I didn't know," Dad says sadly.

"Then you shouldn't have said it was going to be fine!" I shout.

Aunt Miriam and Officer Wentzel are watching me, waiting for me to answer some questions about other incidents I had witnessed between Dad and Mr. Vance. Questions about whether the person who had run out the door had said anything when he'd come in. Whether he'd seemed surprised to see us, like he'd entered our house accidentally.

The policeman and my aunt haven't heard me or Dad speaking. To them, Dad's seat is empty. Even though he's starting to look faded and watery around the edges, to me, the couch is full of him, the smell of his aftershave, his soft brown sweater that has started unraveling. To me, the last four days have been full of him, full of cold.

"There was another incident," Aunt Miriam says, trying to encourage me to tell them more about what happened. "Right, Kemi?"

I nod.

A week after the accident at Grab 'N Pay, a cop knocked on our front door. She asked to speak with Dad. Mr. Vance's house had been robbed, and Mr. Vance had told the cops he thought we had something to do with it. Lo was napping, and as Dad and Mom sat in the living room, talking to the cop, I sat at the top of the stairs and scribbled out some random probabilities in my notebook.

The probability of drawing a queen in a deck of cards: 4/52

The probability of drawing a black queen in a deck of cards: 2/52

The probability of drawing a black queen of spades in a deck of cards: 1/52

I didn't know what would happen with the cop, whether she would believe my parents, but knowing what would happen when I drew from a stack of cards helped. It was something I could predict, and I needed all the things I could predict.

When the cop left, I heaved a giant sigh of relief and hugged my parents.

Now, Officer Wentzel leans forward on the couch, scribbling across the notepad resting on his knee. "It sounds like Mr. Vance had been bothering your family for quite some time."

"Yes," I say.

"Did you see who shot your father, Kemi?"

"Yes," I say, but I can't get the rest of the words out. Not until Dad nods at me and says, "Go on, baby. Be brave."

Him

AFTER I SAW IT—THE STAIN OF RED ON DAD'S CHEST—I stood up and looked toward the front door that I could just make out from the living room. The shooter's face was so different, so twisted up with shock or anger or something else, that I almost didn't recognize him. He turned and ran, but not before I spotted a glint of metal on the ground. I didn't touch it, but when I walked closer, I saw that there were three silver coins on a broken chain. Each coin had a number: *8, 4, 7.*

Officer Wentzel writes this down. He stands.

"Those are all my questions for you, Kemi," he says.

He doesn't say if he thinks Mr. Vance thought he was entering his own house, like Mr. Vance says he did. He doesn't tell me if Mr. Vance will be punished for the things that happened four days ago or the things that have been happening for more than a year.

He says, "I'm sorry about the loss of your father. He seemed like a good man."

I stand too. "Thank you," I say.

Dad squeezes my shoulder. "Atta girl," he whispers, even though he doesn't need to. No one can hear him anyway.

Aunt Miriam shows Officer Wentzel out, then comes back into the room and hugs me.

"I'm so sorry this is happening, Kemi," she says. "But I want you to know that you did a really courageous thing today, and I'm proud of you. Your dad would be so proud of you."

"He is," I say before I can stop myself.

Aunt Miriam gives me a strange look, then she nods.

"Will you go get ready? We're running late and we need to be in the car in the next fifteen minutes."

My heart drum rolls in my chest as I go upstairs to get changed, to put on the outfit I will be wearing when the world ends.

ONE HOUR
Until the End of the World

Dying Things

DAD STAYS DOWNSTAIRS WHILE I GO UP TO TILLIE'S ROOM and get changed. I pull the black garment bag Dia gave me out of the closet, put it on the bottom bunk, and unzip it.

It is a beautiful dark blue dress with beading around the waist and a belt. It is not too *Dia* like I was afraid it might be—over-the-top and fancy and too bright. It is just right.

I slip it on over my head, feeling the soft fabric between my fingers. I almost don't want to wear it, it's so beautiful. I think it's one of Dia's never-worn dresses, the ones she buys at vintage stores and saves for the perfect special occasion. Does the end of the world count as a special occasion? Is the last of everything special just because it's last?

I put on the black shoes I usually wear for church that Mom brought over in my backpack full of clothes four days ago.

When I finish dressing, downstairs is bustling. Uncle Steve is calling for everyone to get in the car. Jen is finishing Tillie's hair, and Grandma is holding Lo and checking that all the stoves are off. Mom comes downstairs quietly. She looks so much older and even though her pregnant tummy makes her dress fit different than it normally does, she somehow looks small. Her eyes are red too, like she's cried for three days straight.

She doesn't say anything to me, but she threads her hand in mine.

Dad shows up now too. He moves so slowly that I can almost hear his bones creak. He coughs, then smiles at me. "That is some dress, Grit."

I can't smile back.

We walk out to the driveway and to Uncle Jeremiah's car. Me, Dad, and Mom. The way it always is. The way it always was.

Mom gets into the car, but before I can, Tillie runs up to me.

She pushes something into my hand and closes it into a fist.

When I open my hand, her yellow (now mostly brown)

flower is in my palm. My first reaction is annoyed. If Tillie knew she didn't want to keep it, why didn't she put it in the time capsule? Why didn't she throw it away like normal people do with dead flowers?

"Tillie, this is useless." I finally say what everyone is thinking, and my voice is sharp around the edges, like a piece of glass. "I can't do anything with it."

I don't know what use I have for another dying thing and I almost toss it down right there on the grass next to the car.

"I know," she says. "But you can have it."

"No." *I don't want it,* I start to say, thinking she has misunderstood me. But then I hear the words again, and *have* suddenly sounds like *love* and *keep* and *save.* It sounds like *carry,* that word that means to bear the weight of and hold and protect. It sounds like *here is a thing you can* carry *that reminds you that someone loves you.* Some things have no use; they are just there to have.

I wonder if this is what Tillie was saving it for all along, if this is why she hasn't put the flower in her miscellaneous box all this time, if it was always going to be different from all her other things with no use. A gift.

"Thank you," I say, and my voice is a quiet whisper, round like the shape of a secret.

Tillie runs away and I have her flower.

I decide that when the world ends, I might need something to hold on to. Something that is just as delicate and broken as me. When you're someone's favorite person and they give you a thing right before the apocalypse and they might have special X-ray vision for recognizing extraordinary things, it is probably precious enough to keep. So I stick it in the pocket of my dress.

The sky is deep purple again, threatening and dark. The asteroid is closer than it has ever been. It is minutes from crushing us, seconds from grounding us to a pulp.

I slide into the car beside Mom. Dad slides in beside me. Uncle Jeremiah drives to the last place where we are ever going to be together, to the place where the world ends.

TWENTY MINUTES
Until the End of the World

Acceleration

WE DRIVE RIGHT INTO IT, INTO THE EPICENTER OF AMPLUS-68.

It is not just going to come to us; we are going to meet it.

It is going to be a collision. Our car and the asteroid going full speed at each other until we crash.

SEVEN MINUTES
Until the End of the World

Collision

UNCLE JEREMIAH DRIVES AROUND A BEND.

I hold Mom's hand and tighten my grip on Dad's as my heart gallops like a racehorse in my chest. The sky goes darker and darker and darker until it's impossible to see anything in front of or around us.

THREE MINUTES
Until the End of the World

Point of Contact

TIRES PEELING AGAINST THE ASPHALT.

Heart thumping now-now-*now*.

The roar of noise as we get closer, closer, closer . . .

ONE MINUTE
Until the End of the World

Explosion

WE ARE SECONDS AWAY FROM IMPACT, AND BECAUSE I AM always thinking about numbers, I count.

One.

The earth rumbles.

Two.

A crash.

Three.

The world explodes.

IMPACT

How It Actually Ends

I ALWAYS THOUGHT THE WORLD WOULD END WITH A BANG. (Not with a hissing sound or no sound, like my other theories said it could.) I always thought the world would end with a massive explosion and the earth quaking and buildings crumbling like a deck of cards. But the actual end of the world is the sound of a car pulling to a stop in front of a church. It is car doors opening and shutting one after the other. *Bang. Bang. Bang.*

It is me burying my face in my mother's dress and whispering, "I can't" over and over again, because today we are supposed to bury my father.

It is Mom cradling my face in her hands and saying, her voice fierce, "Yes, you can, baby. You can." There are tears dripping down her face.

Grandma brings Lo over and Mom puts my sister on her hip. My legs feel like jelly as we walk into the church.

My cousins surround me, hugging me and holding my hand.

We walk by mourners and protesters. People with the same signs from our street in Pineview.

"JUSTICE FOR CARTER" and "BLACK LIVES MATTER" and "MURDER IS A CRIME" and "EVEN OUR HOMES AREN'T SAFE."

The mourners are different from the news reporters who ambushed me and Lucas, but these people were there too the day Jen drove me and Lucas to my house.

They chant Dad's name. "*Ja-red, Ja-red!*" Some of them are crying.

I can't look at them.

Inside, I see Mrs. Sorensen on the left side of the church.

I see Dia in a middle pew between her moms, but I am too sad to wave at her.

When I sit on a hard wooden pew beside Mom, Dad appears on my right. He smells right, but he still looks like that thinner, gray-skinned, murky version of himself.

"I'm here," he promises me now. I take his hand.

The pastor starts speaking, saying things about Dad's life, about his faith in God and people. Uncle Steve gets up too and gives a eulogy, but I'm only barely listening.

I start crying halfway through Uncle Steve's speech.

"What is it, Grit?" Dad whispers to me, even though he doesn't need to. No one can hear or see him.

"I never found it," I say. "Your memento. The thing you would have wanted to put in the box."

"It was never up to you to find it," Dad says. "You have nothing to feel bad about."

"I promised I would!" I insist, because it was my job to remember and save the thing Dad loved the most. And I failed. My *stupid* experiment. The useless data I collected that only figured out that Dad didn't crazy-love basketball, renovations, baking, or the stars.

"Now you'll never know the thing you loved the most," I say, so sad my heart feels huge and tight.

"I do know what it was, though," he says, and that surprises me so much that I swivel my head to face him.

"You *do*?"

"Yes," Dad says. "It was the last thing I thought of. When I took my last breath, I realized what my passion was.

"It's your mom when she's concentrating so hard on a painting that she burns dinner, when there's paint on her nose and on her hands and her neck and even in her hair. And she doesn't even know it's there, never mind know how it got there!" Dad says, and he's grinning so wide that it makes my chest hurt. "It's Lo with her big, loud personality. For a long time, our family felt finished with just you, me, and your mother. After losing Ty, we were scared to try again in case it went wrong, but Lo pushed her way right into our family. She made us have to speak louder and reach higher for things on the shelves. She made us sleep less, made us more awake. And after that, we thought, *maybe we have enough love for even one more.* So now there's Z."

Dad got choked up as he spoke. "My goodness, do I want to meet her. I think I will, but for now I don't know who she's going to be. I'm never going to hold her or know her favorite food or see her graduate one day, but she's making our family complete.

"It's you, Grit. The way your face lights up when you learn a new scientific fact or the way you crinkle your nose when you're thinking hard, solving a probability problem. It is the way you have my laugh and the fact that we can watch ten hours of someone rushing or crushing a house and never get bored. It is dancing around the kitchen with you or your sister on my feet. It is reading bedtime stories to Lo and burning pancakes with you, feeling Z do gymnastics and talking to your mother first thing in the morning. That's what I love with all of my heart. The four of you. If I had chosen my last words, it would have been this: *My girls*. My beautiful, strong, smart girls."

I am crying again now. Big, jerky hiccups. "If you'd worn the forever T-shirt, maybe the magic would have protected you," I say.

"Maybe it would have," Dad agrees softly, "but I wasn't wearing it and it didn't protect me. And as much as it hurts, we have to accept the truth. The facts of the situation."

It sounds like something I could have said. The facts are the most important thing.

"It's not fair, Daddy," I say, crying in a way I haven't since I was a baby. "You don't deserve to be dead. You deserve to be alive and here."

"Well, there's one thing I can promise you, Grit. As long as you're here, as long as the people I love most are here, I will be too. I will *always* be with you." He pats his chest. "In here."

"I want you out here!" I say, gesturing around the room. "I want you waking me up for school and helping me with probability problems and looking at the stars with me. I want you *here*. In my heart is not good enough."

Dad's eyes are filling now too. I think he's going to say something about how this is all we have and we should make the best of it, but all he says is, "I know, honey. It's the worst thing in the world."

"We're not us without you. How will we ever be a family again? Mom stays in bed all day, crying."

My words sound all choppy and tight.

"This is the hardest thing your mother has ever gone through. Yes, it has put her under a lot of stress and into a lot of pain. But your mom is going to be okay, Grit," he promises. "She just needs time."

He sounds just as sure as when Mom said, "I will be here as long as you need me." And maybe he knows something I don't. Maybe they both do.

"Z isn't going to ever know you," I point out, pressing my palm into my wet cheeks.

"Sure, she will," Dad says. "There're pictures and videos, and you'll tell her all about me." He nudges my shoulder and jokes. "Tell her just the good things, okay?"

But I am too upset to smile.

"What about Lo, though? Lo is cranky and tired," I say, and then I admit, "I am so sad that I want to curl up in a hole and never come out. We need you to be *us*."

"Is that what the asteroid has been about?" Dad asks. "Because if I'm not here, we won't be us—the Spectaculars—anymore?"

I stare down at my lap. "When it happened . . ." I can't

bring myself to say the words: *when you died*. But that's what I mean. "It felt so big and so awful that I couldn't imagine it being anything other than the end of the world. It felt like we would all die with you. Maybe not right away, but at least when we had to bury you. When we had to say good-bye forever."

"And the time capsule," Dad says. It's a question that isn't a question.

"Everything in there was for you. Our favorite mementos of you," I say.

I think of the stories each of my family members told me about Dad when they handed me their memento. The socks Dad lent Uncle Steve on his wedding day, the OPEN sign Dad gave Jen after she taught him how to braid hair on my doll, Ella, and he told her she would start her own salon. The kuli kuli Grandma always made especially for Dad, the boarding pass Uncle Jere kept from their trip. Unique, the stuffie Dad rescued out of a big street trash can after Lucas accidentally threw it away. The *everything* Mom wanted to save that reminded her of all of us. Lo's stuffie that Dad brought home from one of his trips. The menu from Patricia's Diner that was the start of Mom and Dad and our family. Tillie's note that just simply said: *I love you*.

"We're going to die without you, Dad," I tell him again because it's true. Who will be the first to suggest sing-offs?

Who will drive me to school and back? Who will be an expert on me, if not him? Who will ask me probability problems just to make me happy?

Science says that humans need oxygen, water, food, and warmth to survive, but for the first time in my life, I think science is wrong.

I'm pretty sure I need my father's laugh, identical to mine, to breathe. I need his strong hands and his kind eyes to stay warm. I need his way of dancing when "his jam" comes on to be full inside. I need him now, and I'll always need him.

Dad leans down so his face is close to mine.

"You won't die without me, Grit," he says, his voice just as fierce as Mom's was earlier. "You know why? Because you have this strength, this thing inside you—a will to survive. Ever since you were a baby, it's been there."

I sniff as he keeps talking. "You're strong. And you're brave. And I know you'll miss me, but your life isn't over. It's not the end of the world."

He squeezes my hand. "I promise. And that's why I said before, why I've kept saying, that you'll be okay. Because you will. It will always be sad and unfair that this happened, but it won't break you. Not you, Grit."

A tear plops onto the knee of my dress. "I'm scared," I tell Dad. "I'm so, so scared. What if he comes back for us?

What if Mom and everybody I know dies? I don't know how to be brave." The world has always felt scary to me, but from the moment that gunshot sounded, I knew the world would never feel safe again. I will always know that people can be evil, that death is quick and final. I will always see my father's eyes open, the blood gushing out in a pool around him. I will always hear my mother's scream. I will always feel that moment of panic when I don't know if Lo has been shot too, if the shooter will shoot again, if my universe will survive, if it won't.

"I can't promise you nothing bad will ever happen again. I wish I could, but I can't," Dad says. "But my job and your job isn't to see life coming. It's to be the best you can be, to love people, to live even if it scares you. That's the thing I want most for you—not that you stop being afraid, but that you keep living, even when you're afraid."

I swipe my hand underneath my eyes.

"Can you do something for me?" Dad asks now.

I nod, because I will do anything for him. Because he is my favorite person in the universe. Because if fathers can be best friends, he is mine, and even if they can't, he is mine.

"Can you take care of your mom and my baby girls for me?" Dad asks, his voice breaking in the middle. "They're going to need you and you're going to need them, and I want you to promise me that even when I'm gone, you will still be the Spectaculars."

"Not without you, Dad," I say in a tiny voice, a pleading voice, because I know what he's saying.

"I'll always be the Sleep Bandit and I'll always be *one* of you, but I can't be here the way I want to be. Remember what I said that day when we looked at the stars? People get closer or farther away, but they don't leave. I'm going to be a little farther away, so you have to be strong and wonderful and wise and silly and everything you are without me. You have to be Statgirl. That's what will make me happiest of all."

I wipe my nose on the sleeve of my dress.

"Promise me," Dad says like it is the most urgent thing of all.

"I promise," I whisper.

"That's my girl," he says.

And then he looks down between us to where I've been clinging to his hand. He lets his almost see-through hand loosen around mine and I start crying again.

No no no no no.

"Please don't leave me," I whisper.

"Not ever," Dad says, smiling a little. "You don't need to see me to know I'm still here."

I can tell the service is almost done by the way people are shuffling in their seats, the fact that the pastor is saying a prayer. But right then, something strange happens. On my left, in Mom's lap, Lo sticks out her hand to me.

Feeling my chest hurt so much that it feels like it will explode, I let go of Dad's hand and grip Lo's tiny one.

I hold it for the rest of the service.

I hold it when I look to my right and there is now a small space between me and Grandma, and no one else between us.

I hold it when Uncle Steve plays the song he chose to be the last song, one about forever and saying goodbye.

If you want to know how the world actually ends, it ends with that song.

After it, my father is gone, the kind of gone that never changes.

Not the kind of gone that is leaving for a trip.

The kind of gone that means he will never hold my hand again or smile his crinkly smile or talk about probability with me or watch *Rush It or Crush It* with me again.

It is the worst kind of gone. The most final type of gone, like an asteroid smashing everything to bits.

Like a supernova that explodes and burns up all the other stars, the whole family of stars.

Like the end of the world.

The Monty Hall Problem (Part I)

On the way home from the funeral, I think of the Monty Hall Problem.

The Monty Hall Problem is one of the most famous problems in the history of statistics.

It goes like this: You're on a game show, and you have to choose between three doors. Behind one door is a car; behind the other two, there are goats. Obviously, you want to win the car and not a goat.

You pick the door you think has the car—let's say door number 1—and then the host, Monty Hall, who knows what's behind the doors, opens door number 3 to show you that it has a goat.

Now, he asks you, "Do you want to change your answer and switch to door number 2? Or will you stick with door number 1?"

The correct answer is that you *should* switch to door number 2.

The probability that the car was behind door number 1 was 1/3. But when Monty picks door 3 to show you, this gives you new information and tells you the car is *probably not* behind door 1. It also tells you that the car is *more likely* behind door 2, because otherwise Monty, knowing what's behind all the doors, would have picked that door.

I can't really fully wrap my head around this problem because some things are just like that, too big to wrap your mind around. But what I understand about it is that, in statistics and in life, you have to pay attention to new information.

The Monty Hall Problem (Part II)

Aғᴛᴇʀ ᴛʜᴇ ғᴜɴᴇʀᴀʟ, ᴡᴇ ʜᴀᴠᴇ ᴛʜᴇ ᴡᴀᴋᴇ ᴀᴛ Aᴜɴᴛ Mɪʀɪ-
am's house.

This means that the house is full of strangers and people
I know, people who loved and knew Dad. There is jollof
rice and plantain and all the other foods Grandma has spent
the last couple of days making. Dia comes over for a while
with her moms. She is wearing the simplest black dress I've
ever seen her in, with just a dab of *Dia* in the long shawl
she wears over it. She hugs me and tells me she loves me
and that her dress looks great on me. Dia and I carry plates
of food that we're not going to eat and settle next to each
other on the stairs.

"I have something to admit," Dia blurts out. "I wanted
to go to school."

"What?" I say, confused.

"You know how I said my moms made me go? Well, they did, but I wanted to as well," she says, fiddling with her fork.

"But you don't like school," I point out.

"Yeah, well," she sighs. "I thought maybe I could give my attendance points to you and you could still have as many points as Lindsay P."

"Wow," I say, and I know without a doubt that it is the kindest thing anyone has done for me. "Thanks, Dia."

She shrugs. "That's what best friends do, right? My points are your points. My end-of-the-world dress is your end-of-the-world dress. Your asteroid is my asteroid."

Dia's words make me want to cry with a warm feeling that, for the first time today, isn't sadness. So I just nod.

She lets out another puff of breath. "Anyway, Mr. Gracen said no to sharing attendance points *and* to the cravat. I really think he'll regret it when I'm famous."

Dia plans to be famous in ten or fifteen years, but in this moment, I wonder how she can even plan that far ahead, how she can see anything but the next second in front of her. I keep forgetting to continue breathing.

"What are you thinking?" she asks quietly, looking over at me.

I tell her about how my chest is so heavy with sadness that it keeps getting tight, trapping all the air in my lungs, and suddenly I can never seem to remember whether I'm on *in* or *out*.

"Just choose one. In *or* out," she suggests. "You have 50 percent chance of being right anyway, right?"

I look at Dia in shock because her math is totally correct and because she just solved a really big problem with probability.

Dia hugs me and leaves as even more visitors arrive.

When she's gone, Lucas and Tillie find me and stick close, like a pair of guard dogs, but people keep coming up to me anyway. Hugging me and grabbing my hands, talking about praying for justice, saying, "Sometimes life just isn't right" and "I'm sorry for your loss" and "Your dad would be so proud of you."

They are trying to make me feel better, but I feel tired and heavy, like I have been climbing a million stairs. Most of all, I feel sad. I think maybe it's the way Mom has felt all along, why she's been in bed.

I stick close to Mom. Mom sticks close to Lo. We are like a human train, all of us trying to stay close to each other.

Lo seems to feel as tired as I do because she starts wailing about halfway through the wake. Mom tries to soothe her and bumps her on her hip and says comforting words to her, but Lo isn't listening. I kind of wish that I were as little as she is, that I could just scream my lungs out to show my sadness. It isn't enough to wear black or eat jollof rice or hug each other and talk about Dad. I want to cry and cry and not let anybody comfort me, because the only person who can is gone.

Mom finally gets Lo to fall asleep and she takes her upstairs.

While she's gone, Mom's friend Susan tells me about the time Dad helped her change her flat tire.

"He was such a good man," she says, and I am happy that everyone seems to think this of Dad, but sad that somehow good men can still be murdered in their own living room.

I touch Tillie's dead flower in my pocket while Susan talks and then I realize it's been a super long time and Mom isn't back from tucking Lo in.

"I'm going upstairs to check on Mom," I tell my bodyguards, Lucas and Tillie.

"We'll come too!" Tillie says.

"It's okay. I'll be right back," I say.

The truth is, as much as I love Lucas and Tillie, I'm a little tired of their attention too. I go into the guest room Mom and Lo have been sharing the past four days. The curtains are pulled shut and Mom is lying next to Lo.

"Honey?" she says.

And for a second, I wonder whether she thinks I'm Dad.

It makes me want to cry.

"It's Kemi," I say.

"I know," Mom says. She sits up in bed. It feels like she has been in this bed every minute since Dad died. I don't know if she will ever get out again.

"I'm sorry that I left you down there. I'm just so, so tired. I couldn't take another minute of being hugged or touched or looked at."

I know exactly what she means.

"Plus, why do people always think they can touch a pregnant woman's belly without asking?" She makes a face. Mom is talking in a whisper, so we don't wake Lo.

I sit on the edge of her bed and stare straight ahead at the door.

Dad said in the church that we would be okay without him, but I don't think it's true. If our family were those stars on the ceiling in my room, we have burned out.

"What happens to stars when they die?" I ask Mom.

"They turn into something else. Either a black hole or a neutron star."

I've heard of black holes before, but I haven't heard of neutron stars.

"So they're just big dead rocks?" I say.

"Actually, no, if I remember correctly," Mom says. "But I might not be. Wanna look it up with me?"

302

I climb up on the bed, squeezing in between Mom and Lo. We use Mom's phone to look it up. Sometimes I forget Mom likes facts and research just as much as I do. Sometimes I forget that I am half of her too. That I am made up of art and colors and singing and Yoruba, just like Mom is.

Suddenly, I want Mom to know that I remember that I am part of her too. Because I can't imagine her losing Dad and also thinking that I'm not glad she's here. What if the sadness of Dad's death kills her and she dies not knowing how much I love her? So I say, "I love you more than all the theories in the world."

"I love you more than everything I love," she says, and *whoa*. I feel the hugeness of it, like a giant wave covering me, as Mom wraps an arm around my shoulder and holds me close. She goes back to looking at her phone.

"Neutron stars and black holes are some of the most exotic objects in the universe," Mom reads out loud. "If you took a teaspoon of neutron star matter it would weigh as much as all of humanity."

I know Mom expects me to be impressed but I just nod. "And black holes?"

"A region of space where matter is so compact that nothing can escape from it. Not even light," Mom reads.

I think about the heavy sadness on my chest that feels as big as the whole world, and I wonder if I have fallen into a black hole. Maybe that's what has happened. The asteroid has hit and the Earth has become a giant black hole, and there will never be anything bright or light again. There will be no escaping from it.

I sigh.

So stars die and become nothing? Why are endings so horrible and final and sad?

"Stars become something different," Mom corrects me, and it reminds me a little of the end of the world, the fact that humans can become dust or stars or water or trees. It reminds me that even if the world ends, there will always be an after.

"Today—this week," Mom says, her eyes filling a bit. "It's been one of the saddest, hardest days and weeks ever."

"Nothing is ever going to be the same again," I say, staring down at my lap as everything blurs.

"I know," Mom says, her voice shaky. "I miss your father so much that sometimes I feel stuck. Like I physically cannot move or eat or do much of anything. "

I nod, look down at the comforter.

"But I'm not going anywhere, Kemi. I'm grieving. I'm *sad*. And that will probably never change, but I'm going to keep going for my girls, my babies."

I think of what Dad wanted his final words to be: *My girls.*

Now, Mom says something I don't expect. "I'm more than just sad. I'm determined. I'm resilient. I'm angry too. Angry as heck that someone would hurt your father for such a stupid reason or for absolutely no reason at all. Because he never thought we belonged there, so of course *we* were in *his* house. I'm angry that whatever happens to the man who did this will not be nearly as bad as what has happened to us. I'm not going to tell you that it will get any less painful or any less hard, but we will get through it," Mom says.

Even though Dad said the same thing to me in the church before he left, I can't understand how she can say we will get through this.

Dad is *gone*.

Dead.

Never coming back.

It is the worst thing. The very worst thing in the world.

"We'll get through it together," Mom says, turning so she can look me in the eye. "You and me and Lo and Zaria."

"Zaria," I repeat, eyes wide but still full of sadness.

"It's a city in Nigeria," Mom says, "but some people also say it means a blooming flower. Other people say it means radiance."

And *whoa*, I think.

"Radiant like a star?"

"Radiant like a star," Mom confirms.

And I understand that even before they meant to, Mom and Dad made a promise to Z. And to me and Lo.

We'll always be stars.

I want to be happy, want to be excited, but something holds me back.

"Statistically, men are supposed to live to be seventy. If he hadn't been shot, he would probably have lived thirty more years." I looked this up too, on Monday. Dad was thirty-nine.

Mom wraps her arm around me and squeezes me to her side. "I know," she says. "But do we know that for sure? That he would have lived to be seventy?"

"Kemi?" Mom says.

"No," I mumble.

Probability tells you what is likely to happen, not what *will* happen.

"You know, your father was so proud of you," she says. "He thought you were so brave and could do absolutely anything you set your mind to."

"Like become a scientist?" I say, feeling a hopeful little kick in my chest.

"Like anything," Mom says.

Then I remember about the funeral and the shooting and the way the universe can explode. My shoulders slump down, and my hands start trembling.

"I don't think I want to be anything anymore," I tell Mom. I don't want to be strong or brave. I don't want to be Grit. "I just want Dad back. That's all I want."

My voice cracks and then I'm crying, big breathless tears, and Mom hugs me to her chest and I hear her crying into my hair too.

Finally, without letting go, she whispers, "You don't have to be strong, baby. We'll do it weak. We'll limp and hurt and take everything one day at a time.

"If it helps, though," Mom adds, "you couldn't convince your father that you were anything *but* a survivor. A trier."

My father thought I was strong and special and so many other things. He thought I was like Piper Peters from *Rush it or Crush it*. That when the chips were down, I would look to the camera with determined eyes and set shoulders and say, "I'm not going down without a fight."

Today is the saddest day of my life and I don't feel like fighting.

But I figure, if Dad believed so much in me, then I can at least try.

I can try to be as strong as he believed I was.

I can try to be as brave as he thought I was.

Mom and I lie down on the bed, the three of us (plus Z) curled up together in the dark room. She tells me that Lucas brought the time capsule in from the rain, that we can bury it together sometime.

Even with the baby who is going to be parts of Dad and parts of Mom and parts of something totally herself, even with all of that, it feels like the three of us are missing something big and vital, like a stomach or a heart or a lung. But somehow, we are alive.

I sit up again because I realize there is a question I never got around to asking, some research I haven't done.

Mom lets me use her phone again and I just sit there, staring in the dark at the screen in disbelief, because I hadn't expected this.

But all along? It turns out that stars are bigger than asteroids. If you play rock, paper, scissors with asteroids and stars, stars trump asteroids.

I think about the Monty Hall Problem. It is new information to me that *stars trump asteroids*, but it changes everything. And I can't ignore it. The lesson from the Monty Hall Problem is to always consider new information.

We are stars: Mom, Dad, Lo, Zaria, and me.

The asteroid: Dad's death, Dad's funeral.

The new information?

We—Mom, Dad, Lo, Zaria, and me—are bigger than the thing that came and knocked us out of the sky.

We can survive it.

We *will* survive it.

Grit

WE MUST SLEEP STRAIGHT THROUGH THE REST OF THE wake, because when I open my eyes the next morning, I'm still in Mom and Lo's bed. In Aunt Miriam's guest room.

The room smells like something chemical and so familiar that, for the first time in days, I feel like I might be home.

Through my blurry eyes, I see an easel set up in one corner of the room. Mom is painting again.

Lo is asleep beside me, but I hear Mom's voice downstairs.

I climb out of bed and find her at the bottom of the stairs, talking to Aunt Miriam.

"I want to go to the rally," Mom is saying, clutching the

strap of the bag on her shoulder. She has a quiet strength in her voice, and she's rubbing her belly absently.

"These people have supported us, protested for days, and taken up our cause," Mom says.

I know she is talking about the people who were protesting on our street in Pineview, the people who were outside the church yesterday. The people who have signed petitions and written letters and haven't treated us the way most people in Pineview did. Even though Mom and I told the truth about what happened, there are lots of people who are saying that Mr. Vance was a good guy, that he shouldn't be punished for accidentally going into the wrong house and shooting when he heard a noise. Even some of the cops have said that Mr. Vance shouldn't be punished.

"I'm just not sure you're up to it," Aunt Miriam says, "but if you insist, I'll go with you."

"I want to go too," I hear my own voice saying, loud and clear from the top of the stairs.

Mom and Aunt Miriam look up.

You're allowed to fight for that world; you're allowed to make waves, Dad said.

"Honey, I didn't know you were awake. It's still early," Mom says.

"Stay home and hang out with Luc and Tillie," Aunt Miriam says, but I don't budge. They want me to be in summer mode, lazy and sleepy and doing the least amount of everything, but I want to be as strong as Dad thought I was.

"I want to go to the rally," I say.

"That's a hard, hard thing to do, Kemi," Mom says. "There'll be reporters and crowds, and I just don't think you're old enough."

"Yes, I am," I say. Mom and Dad never let me watch movies with violence, but I saw my father die. If I am old enough for that, then I'm old enough for a rally too.

Mom thinks about it for a second. She bites her lower lip.

"Okay, baby," she says. "Let's go."

She holds out her hand and I go down the stairs and take it.

The Truth

Dear Reader/Alien/Earthling,

The probability that you are angry with me right now must be close to 100 percent.

I told you that I was going to tell you the important facts and then I lied.

Except I didn't really.

I mean, I did but not about everything.

Here is a list of the details that are true, facts you can find anywhere, things you can prove:

* My name is Kemi Carter and I'm eleven.

* I have a sister named Lola, a mother named Bim, and I'm going to have a sister called Zaria.
* I had a father named Jared.
* I am a scientist.
* I researched all the facts about asteroids and put them together to make up AMPLUS-68.
* I love probability because it helps predict the world.
* I saw my father get murdered one Sunday morning.

A list of things you will not be able to prove because I only wanted them to be true, but they were not:
* There was an asteroid in the sky.
* We had four days before the asteroid collided with Earth.
* Dad spent the four days at Aunt Miriam's with us.

A list of things you might not be able to prove, even though they are true:
* My dad was my best friend in the world.
* Watching him die was like watching the world crash into something massive and fiery and unstoppable.

* The asteroid was Dad's funeral, the moment we would say goodbye to him, and it kept growing closer and closer every second.
* I couldn't let go of my father.
* And then I did.

I am sorry I lied to you. I know you are most likely an alien and may or may not speak English (I say the chances are pretty slim that you do), but I hope you know why I did it. I hope you know that my father was so great and so kind and so funny that when he died, it felt like the worst thing in the world. The thing we couldn't survive. The end of the world.

In some ways, it will always feel like that because my sisters and I no longer have a father.

We will never see his smile again or hear his voice or watch TV with him. Zaria will never know that to have a dad is to feel him holding your bike steady as you learn to ride. She will never know the scratchiness of his beard on her face or the pads of his big feet under her own feet as he dances her across the kitchen and sings off-key about purple rain. Mom no longer has a husband.

It was the worst thing.

It is the worst thing.

But I realized something: the world only ends when the world ends.

And even then, there's an after.

Something else I realized: asteroids and meteorites and other falling objects collide with Earth all the time.

Mostly, they are survivable.

They can harm things and change things and even kill things, but they have not ever destroyed the entire world.

And probably, they never will.

THE PROBABILITY OF EVERYTHING

The odds of finding a pearl in an oyster
—1 IN 12,000

The odds of being struck by lightning over a
lifetime
—1 IN 3,000

The odds of winning the lottery
—1 IN 300 MILLION

The odds of getting hit by a meteorite
—1 IN 3,000

The odds of winning an Olympic gold medal
—1 IN 662,000

The odds of being ambidextrous (being able to use
your right and left hand)
—1 IN 100

The odds of being born on Leap Day
—1 IN 1,461

317

The odds of being born
—1 IN 5.5 TRILLION

The odds of dying on any given day
—1 IN 365 (NORMAL YEAR) OR 1 IN 366 (LEAP YEAR)

The odds of dying from a gunshot in America
—1 IN 315

The probability that my father is coming back
—0%

The probability that everything has changed
—100%

The probability that we will keep fighting for the world we want, and the probability that we will make waves
—100%

The probability that there is always an after
—100%

Author's Note

WHEN I WAS A KID, MY FAVORITE UNCLE DIED IN THE room across the hall from mine. As I remember it, he had been sick for a couple of days before, but I was sure he would recover. People always recovered. Except . . . he didn't. Waking up that morning, hearing that he was really and truly gone, never coming back, was one of the most devastating and shocking moments of my life. Especially because, at the time, no one really talked with me about his death—why he died and what it meant that he was gone.

This book was always going to be about that type of grief, a grief that feels surreal and impossible to wrap your mind around. But as I wrote, I started to grieve a new kind of loss. I heard about Botham Jean, an unarmed Black man who was shot and killed by an off-duty officer in his own home. I heard about Breonna Taylor, a young Black woman who was shot and killed by police in her apartment while she slept. I heard about George Floyd, another unarmed Black man who was killed by police.

As I write this, just over a month has passed since a mass shooting in Buffalo took the lives of ten Black people and injured three others. The alleged shooter, motivated by hate and misinformation, drove hundreds of miles to intentionally target a community of Black and brown people.

These injustices are some of the things that I grieve over now, as an adult. These are some of my asteroids.

I think often about the people who knew and loved the victims of the Buffalo attack. I think about the people who loved Botham and Breonna and George, people for whom the world is now slightly less real and less beautiful and less fair. Their mothers, their fathers, their children, their best friends. I think about George Floyd's daughter, Gianna, who was just six when her father was killed.

I can't speak for the people who loved these victims, but I felt it was important to tell this story about a family living with the gaping hole of a missing loved one. Both when grief is tied to injustice and when it is not, discussing death and loss is important. We honor those we have lost when we talk about their lives, but it also helps us to move forward. As Kemi learns, there is something that comes after such giant loss, after such terrible sadness and shock and pain. There is an After that can be filled with hope and joy and living with the memories of those who are no longer here. Most importantly, we can honor those we have lost by working for a more just world, by telling their stories, by making waves.

Resources

ACCORDING TO THE UNITED STATES DEPARTMENT OF JUS-tice, hate crimes have been on the rise over the last few years. This is a trend that has been observed in Canada, New Zealand, Russia, Italy, the UK, and Brazil. In 2020, more than 60% of reported hate crimes in the US were race or ethnicity-based.

If you are the victim of a hate crime:

If you are in danger, dial your country's emergency code (e.g., 911) for immediate help.

Report the hate crime to your local police.

- Make sure you record what happened in as much detail as possible soon after the crime.
- File a police report and keep a copy for your personal records.
- If your local police is unhelpful, file a report at the federal level (i.e., the local FBI).
- Reach out to a trained counselor and your personal supports (family, friends, spiritual care worker).

United States/Canada

For US: Call or text 1-855-4-VICTIM or chat online with the VictimConnect Resource Center. Visit victim connect.org

For Canada: See if your province has an anti-racism network: e.g., if in British Columbia, you can visit resilienceBC.ca

UK

For UK: Visit gov.uk/report-hate-crime to report a hate crime.

For countries outside the UK, US, and Canada, please visit your local police station and/or report to a trusted and responsible adult.

For anti-racism resources, visit:

- naacp.org/find-resources
- blacklivesmatter.com/resources
- tryingtogether.org/community-resources/anti-racism-tools
- psacunion.ca/anti-racism-resources
- washington.edu/raceequity/resources/anti-racism-resources

Acknowledgments

IT'S BEEN SAID MANY TIMES THAT IT TAKES A VILLAGE TO publish a book, and this has absolutely been the case with *The Probability of Everything*. I am indebted to so many people. Kate Sullivan helped carve a rough, undefined draft into something meaningful and hopeful. My agent, Suzie Townsend, has been an incredible advocate for this book and all my other books and I'm so grateful. My editor, Emilia Rhodes, thank you for believing so much in Kemi's story. I never imagined I'd get to work with you on it (you could say the probability was *low*?), but I'm so glad! Thank you to the entire team at New Leaf, especially Dani Segelbaum, Sophia Ramos and Kendra Coet. Thank you also to the Clarion team: Trish McGinley, Heather Tamarkin, Celeste Knudsen, Vaishali Nayak, Briana Wood, Taylan Salvati, Mimi Rankin, Josie Dallam, and Gretchen Stelter. Thank you to Laylie Frazier for creating a cover that captures Kemi's universe so beautifully.

I have the best friends and family in the world. Most of you don't get this writing thing, but you've still been there every step of the way. You've all heard Kemi's story in some form or other over the past decade—thank you for telling me there was a place for this book.

Thank you to everyone who has read my books and made space for my words on their shelves or in their hearts.

Finally, to everyone who finds themselves dealing with grief or injustice, I really believe there is always an after. Let's keep fighting for it.